Mixing Temptation

Also by Sara Jane Stone

Mixing Temptation

A SECOND SHOT NOVEL

SARA JANE STONE

AVONIMPULSE

An Imprint of HarperCollinsPublishers

Excerpt from *Serving Trouble* copyright © 2016 by Sara Jane Stone.
Excerpt from *Stirring Attraction* copyright © 2016 by Sara Jane Stone.
Excerpt from *This Earl is on Fire* copyright © 2016 by Vivienne Lorret.
Excerpt from *Torch* copyright © 2016 by Karen Erickson.
Excerpt from *Hero of Mine* copyright © 2016 by Codi Gary.

EPub Edition SEPTEMBER 2016 ISBN: 9780062423887

Print ISBN: 9780062423894

Avon, Avon Impulse, and the Avon Impulse logo are trademarks of HarperCollins Publishers.

10 9 8 7 6 5 4 3 2 1

*For Amanda, thank you for opportunity
to write Caroline and Josh's story!*

Acknowledgments

To ALL MY wonderful readers, I have a secret to share with you. Caroline's story was never part of my plan for this series. When I initially proposed this series, I'd planned to keep Caroline and Josh in the background. But some characters demand their own story.

I first met Caroline while writing *Serving Trouble*. I was researching something else and stumbled upon an article about a woman who'd gone AWOL after she was sexually assaulted while serving in the military. I looked for more first-hand accounts and interviews with veterans and active duty women who suffered from MST (military sexual trauma). A feeling of helplessness filled each story. For many, they felt that there was no way out of the situation.

The more I read, the more time I spent with Caroline—I couldn't leave her in the background. She deserved her own story. And I won't lie. This is the hardest story I've ever written. There were so many times when I wondered if another writer could tell it better. I feared I would not be able to do justice to her plight.

I took extra time thanks to my wonderful, supportive editor. Thank you Amanda and everyone at Avon Impulse for allowing me to follow my heart with this story! I also owe my family a debt of gratitude (and cupcakes for the kids when the book releases!) for allowing me to disappear for hours and sometimes days at a time to write.

A huge 'thank you' to Jill Marsal for being the best agent ever (too many reasons to list!). And for negotiating extensions as I tried to find a happy-ever-after to a situation that so rarely results in a positive ending in everyday life.

I also want to give my little street team, Sara Jane's Seducers, a shout-out! I shared my frustrations and sneak peeks with this group of readers. In return, they drove me to finish this story. And to all of the readers on Facebook, Twitter, Goodreads, Amazon and other social media/review sites who took the time to read and review this series, thank you!! I hope you fall in love with Josh and Caroline.

Prologue

NEVER TRUST A man's smile.

The full moon shone down on the small clearing between the fir trees like a spotlight. Positioned high in the Oregon night sky, the beam of light narrowed in on the tall, broad shouldered man with curly red hair. He wore faded blue jeans, a button-down green flannel, which hung open to reveal a white T-shirt, and a smile.

Run.

Caroline Andrews glanced at the tattered black sleeping bag resting on the forest floor. Her backpack sat next to it. But her gun was safely tucked into the waistband of her black cargo pants.

"Evening, ma'am." The greeting slipped through his smiling lips as he raised his right hand. She reached for her weapon. But before her fingertips touched the barrel, the man's fingers brushed his red curls. Caroline slowed her movements. Still, she kept her hand close to her gun, ready to pull it free from her pants if he gave her cause.

Look at that smile . . . You can't trust him.

Once upon a time in a war zone, her commanding officer had smiled at her. She'd mistaken the curve of his mouth for a gesture of friendship, a signal of comradery in a place that chafed at her nerves. They had arrived in Afghanistan on high alert, ready and waiting for an attack. And she'd kept her guard up.

Until that bastard smiled. . .

She'd anticipated violence and pain. She'd met soldiers who'd lost limbs completing ordinary tasks. Driving a truck from point A to point B. Walking across the base they called home. But no one had warned her that her attacker would win her trust first.

Caroline had walked away from her second tour through Afghanistan with all her limbs. But she'd learned that trusting a man's smile led to trouble.

"Evening," she called back, her voice hoarse. She'd spent the past week traveling through the woods, heading north to small-town Oregon. Timber Country. And home to her fellow Marine Noah Tager. Noah didn't smile much since he'd left their unit. But she trusted him. He'd stood up for her. And he would pay for it if she didn't warn him soon.

"I'm sorry," the grinning redhead said. "But you can't camp here. This is private land. No trespassing and all."

"Trespassing," she repeated. After months of evading the cops, she couldn't waltz straight into their grasp, arrested for camping on private land when she thought she was still in the government-owned forest. Not that the police were actively looking for her. But still, there was a federal warrant out for her arrest.

He nodded, his oh-so-suspicious grin fading. "The crew will be here before dawn. We start harvesting in the morning. The BLM hired us."

She nodded. So she'd been right. The Bureau of Land Management owned this section of forest. Not that it mattered now that she'd been discovered.

And his smile vanished completely. "Look, if you're here to protest—"

"No," she said quickly. "I'm heading to Forever. The college town. My friend lives there and I need to find him."

He cocked his head. "You're almost there. In fact, you're a mile, maybe two, from the Forever town line. I'm headed there myself. I could give you a lift. What is your friend's name?"

She could hear the suspicion in his tone even though she'd bet the last twenty-dollar bill in her possession that she looked nothing like your typical protesting hippie, tree-hugger type right now. Although it had been a long time since she'd brushed her hair—she'd forgotten to toss a comb into her pack—and she desperately needed a shower. But while her last deployment had stripped away pieces of herself, she still walked, talked, and stood like a Marine.

"First, I need your word that you won't tell anyone I'm looking for him. Someone is after him—after us—and if anyone learns that I'm here . . . He's already in danger, so I need you to promise."

His red-gold eyebrows lifted. With the moonlight streaming down on his face, she read his wide-eyed look and it said: 'OK, crazy-pants.'

"All right," he said slowly.

"I'm looking for Noah Tager."

His expression blossomed into another smile. "Looks like you got lucky."

"I doubt that," she muttered. Luck had abandoned her the day she took an oath to defend her country.

"We'll chalk it up to coincidence then. My brother is over at Big Buck's right now. I'll give him a call and see if Noah's tending bar tonight." His right hand slipped into his jeans' pocket and his brow furrowed.

"I left my phone in my truck," he explained as he pulled his hand free and took a step back. "I'll grab it. Wait right here. After we give him a call, I'll drive you over."

Accepting a ride from a smiling stranger? Impossible. And she doubted he knew Noah. The pieces fit too perfectly. Logic told her the charming redhead planned to alert the authorities.

Run.

"What did you say your name was again?" he asked.

She debated lying. But if he was telling the truth and if this smiling stranger knew Noah, then he could tell her where to find him. She took a step back and lowered to the ground, keeping her gaze fixed on him while she reached for her backpack. "Caroline. And you don't need to give me a lift. Just tell me where to find him and I'll go there."

"I know I look like the big bad wolf, but you can trust me."

Not the wolf, she thought. If he walked off the pages of a fairy tale, he'd be mistaken for a prince. The savior. The good guy . . . In another lifetime, she might have returned his smile and climbed into his truck.

"No, I can't," she said flatly. "I can't trust anyone."

"Noah can vouch for me," he added, still oozing confidence and carefree charm as if nothing ever went off course in his life. Then he turned his back on her and disappeared into the trees.

I could have shot him in the back.

She would never take out an innocent bystander. Hell, she'd never even taken a life. Yes, she could handle a firearm. But she'd driven and repaired trucks for the Marines. Not a lot of 'shoot to kill' missions when it came to replacing belts and changing tires.

But he'd walked away as if he trusted her, as if he knew she wouldn't retrieve the gun from her waistband and aim it at him.

Once upon a time, she had walked past fear. She'd shouldered her gun and reported for duty. She'd driven roads potentially littered with IEDs. Fighting alongside men twice her size, she had pulled her weight. And sometimes, while she ate a rushed meal and joked with men she'd considered friends, she'd laughed and relaxed into the feeling that she was one of them.

But her fairy tale had veered off course. Her commanding officer had given the big, bad wolf, the fire-breathing dragon, and every other make-believe monster a run for their money. Because rape did not belong in fairy tales. And rape under command, under the order of someone she'd sworn to obey, a man she'd risked her life for? Her reality was a living, breathing nightmare without a happy-ever-after ending in sight.

And she could no longer walk through fear any more than she could march through a forest fire. It held her back, always threatening to consume her. Right now, there was only one way to survive.

Run.

She shouldered her pack. Then she took a knee, rolled up the sleeping bag, and tucked it under her arm. She heard the crunch of leaves. He was coming back. Slowly, she slipped into the forest he'd accused her of trying to protect. But right now, she needed to find Noah and keep him safe. She couldn't rescue the trees. Hell, when all was said and done, she probably couldn't save herself.

Tonight had proved one thing. It was only a matter of time before the past caught up with her. The police, the man who'd raped her—someone would find her. And when they did, they'd take away the only thing she had left—her freedom.

JOSH SUMMERS STOOD in the empty clearing and made a silent promise. Tomorrow, he would apologize to Caroline—if that was even her real name. Of course, he'd have to find her first. In the time it had taken him to return to his truck, she'd run. And replaying their conversation in his mind, he couldn't blame her.

He should have given the mysterious Caroline directions or handed over his cell. He should have asked what she needed from him instead of insisting that she climb into his truck. Heck, if his sister had accepted a ride from a strange man who happened to be wandering the woods at night, he'd question her common sense.

He'd been caught off guard tonight. And yeah, his first thought on seeing a woman camped in a clearing pointed toward *shit, we're going to have a problem with protesting tree-huggers*. Josh didn't have an issue with environmentalists as long as they kept their distance from the tracts of land Moore Timber had been hired to harvest. And in most cases replant. He loved this land. So did the guys who worked alongside him. Hell, his sister was one of the most outspoken supporters of taking the excess from the timber harvests, the limbs that fell to the forest floor, and turning them into biomass fuel.

But he'd run into plenty of protesters before. Some possessed the same lived-in-the-forest-too-long look, but he'd never met one running on pure fear and desperation. And his only excuse for not spotting her blatant fight-or-flight terror?

Even sporting a hairstyle that suggested she'd forgot to pack her hairbrush when she'd selected flight over fight, Caroline's bright green eyes, creamy skin dotted with a few girl-next-door freckles, and heart-shaped face had thrown him. And her bold, don't-fuck-with-me stance had landed him square on his ass.

But shit, the last time that happened he'd ended up in a dead-end relationship. It had taken him months to break free. But he'd done it. Tonight, before he'd walked into the forest to check on the trees, he'd broken up with his girlfriend. He'd lost his head—but thank freaking God not his heart—over the stacked nursing student who moonlighted as a topless waitress. Although sometimes it seemed like her true focus was serving breakfast at the strip club instead of her classes. But Megan had made it clear she wasn't interested in settling down. And when he stepped back and looked at their time together, he couldn't see a future with her.

He was done playing games. And he'd had enough of cute and coy to last a lifetime. When it came to his dream woman, straightforward and honest now topped the list.

And big green eyes...

Don't go there, he thought. The woman in the woods had held back. But he had a hunch she'd been telling the truth about the key facts. Her name was Caroline. She was looking for Noah Tager. She was in trouble. And her problems were bigger than whether they cut the trees or not.

Hadn't he had enough trouble to last him a lifetime? He'd survived a run-in with a big-ass logging hook on the end of a freaking helicopter. The hit to the head had stolen his short-term memory. And the struggle to re-claim it had pushed him pretty damn close to depression.

He pulled out his phone and dialed. "Hey Chad," he said when his brother picked up. "Is Noah working to-night?"

"Yeah," his brother said. "Where are you? We're at the bar waiting for you."

"I'll be there in fifteen. Maybe twenty." He turned and retraced his steps to his truck. "I stopped by the harvest site. Favor for Eric Moore, our awesome boss. And Noah's going to want to hear about what I found."

He ended the call and opened the door to his truck. He glanced over his shoulder one last time. But no sign of her. As soon as they found Caroline, he'd make things right. And he'd bake her a pie. He hadn't met a woman yet who could resist homemade pie coupled with an apology.

Then he'd steer clear of the beautiful, mysterious woman. Life—and a team of doctors—had granted him a second chance. He damn well better make the most of it.

Chapter 1

Fourteen months later. . .

SOMETIMES LIVING LIFE to the fullest involved breaking into his brother's kitchen on a Saturday morning. Though Josh doubted the small-town cops would write him up for B&E seeing as he had a key to the place. Plus, he'd grown up in the old farmhouse, and still lived in the apartment over the barn. And his brother should be resigned to his early morning baking sessions by now. Even though his siblings questioned his motives for delivering pie after pie to a woman who didn't seem all that interested in dating him, that hadn't stopped him from using the kitchen during his downtime.

He'd spent the past year and change sharing his homemade baked goods with the quiet, reclusive Caroline.

From the pecan pie recipe he'd perfected in the aftermath of a logging accident that had left him searching for ways to reclaim his short-term memory, to his first key lime creation covered in whipped cream. Yeah, baking had proven oddly useful.

Josh Summers spread a thick layer of the homemade topping on the pie and tried not to think about covering the woman determined to keep him locked in the 'friend zone' with the leftovers. After what Caroline had been through, well hell, he understood why she needed time. But that didn't keep him from hoping for more—especially since she'd kissed him in the back room of Big Buck's Bar a few months ago.

And then asked him out.

But she never picked a time or place for your first date...

"What are you making?" a familiar voice demanded as the back door to the Summers' family farmhouse slammed shut.

"Testing out a new key lime pie recipe," he told his older sister without looking up from his creation. Katie Summers—no, make that Katie Trulane now that she'd married the number two at Moore Timber, the logging company that also served as their employer—crowded in at his side. Out of the corner of his eye, he caught sight of her long, red ponytail swinging forward and threatening to land in his pie topping.

Of the four siblings, Katie and Josh had inherited their mother's red hair and green eyes. Thankfully, their looks were the only trait she'd passed on to them. Their mom had walked out on her family when Josh was a kid and never looked back. But the Summers siblings stuck together—even at seven in the morning on a freaking Saturday.

"Is that pie for me?" Katie asked hopefully.

"Nah," another all too familiar voice called out. "Josh stopped baking for us months ago. He's still trying to woo his lady friend with sugar."

"Shut up, Chad," Josh muttered. He dipped the spatula into the bowl of whipped cream and then returned it to the pie laden with cream. Josh had woken up early, slipped out of his apartment over the barn and into the farmhouse kitchen with the hope that he'd be in and out before his siblings stormed Brody's home.

"Shouldn't you all be in bed? You're married"—he shot Katie a pointed look—"and you're engaged." He glanced over his shoulder at Chad. "Plus, you don't live here anymore."

If Josh had what his brothers and sister had fought so hard to find—love with the promise of happy-ever-after and homes of their own—he would stay the hell out of Brody's kitchen on a Saturday morning and while away the hours in bed.

"Lena worked the overnight shift last night, so I stayed here," Chad said with a shrug as he headed for the pot of coffee Josh had made upon breaking in. "I heard you banging around down here and thought I'd see if you started the coffee."

"And I have a sixth sense that tells me when a bowl needs to be licked," Katie said. She made a grab for the nearly empty whipped cream bowl. Now four months along with her first child, Katie had bypassed morning sickness in favor of sugar. And she'd appointed herself his designated 'helper' which amounted to licking the bowls then handing them back to him to wash.

Josh swatted her hand away. "I'm not done with that. Why don't you go feed your goats first?"

"Liam volunteered to take care of the animals this morning."

"When you kick a man out of bed at dawn to feed your barn full of rescued animals, it's called coercion," Josh pointed out.

"He offered because Liam is a smart man and he knows I'll be grateful," she shot back. "Now, please, *please* let me lick the bowl."

Josh rescued the last of the whipped cream, spread it on a not-quite-perfect pie, and handed over the bowl. His sister took her treasure to the kitchen table Brody, the oldest brother and their ringleader since the Summers siblings had lost their father to a sudden heart attack, had built.

"Feeding her cravings again?" Brody's deep voice announced his presence in the kitchen.

Well, speak of the devil.

Though Brody has always been the 'Most Likely To Follow the Straight and Narrow' of the siblings.

"This one is not for me," Katie said. "I just get to share in the licking duties."

"Caroline?" Brody asked with a sigh.

Pretending to be preoccupied with his pie, Josh

nodded. He'd listened to dozens of long-winded speeches and participated in countless debates hosted by his nosy siblings about his dead-end relationship with the Big Buck's dishwasher.

She lives over an hour away from Independence Falls.

Josh had shot down Brody's protest by reminding his big brother that he'd fallen for a woman who'd lived on the other side of the country. Of course, Kat—Josh's former doctor and the woman partly responsible for helping Josh reclaim his short-term memory in the wake of the logging accident—now lived upstairs.

It's been a year and you still haven't shared so much as a pizza.

There was a thread of truth to Chad's argument. But Josh had countered with *she prefers my pies.* And he'd left out the fact that they always shared them in the back room of Big Buck's Bar, hidden away from the curious, small-town gossips that peopled Independence Falls and the neighboring university town where Caroline currently lived and worked—Forever, Oregon.

Josh didn't want to talk about the fact that Caroline was technically in hiding. His siblings—apart from Chad who'd been sworn to secrecy—didn't know her full story and Josh planned to keep it that way. And even Chad had never learned the reasons why Caroline had run from her duty to serve her country. If his siblings found out that she'd been attacked by her commanding officer and still feared him, if they learned that there was a warrant out for her arrest . . .

Yeah, his brothers would probably sit on him—with

Katie standing nearby and cheering them on—until Josh agreed to try dating a woman who could to split a damn pizza in public without fear of getting arrested if the local police stopped by to say hello.

"Any luck with your favorite Big Buck's employee?" Chad asked.

"Mind your own business." Josh took a step back and examined his creation. It screamed homemade and key lime was sure as hell an odd choice for fall in Oregon, but Josh had wanted to try something new.

"But you, baby brother, are my business," Chad said, adding a heavy dose of melodrama to his voice. "And I'm worried about you. When was the last time you got laid?"

Fourteen months ago. . .

"Also none of your business," Josh said as he opened the fridge and set the pie inside.

"I'm just saying maybe you should rethink your strategy," Chad said. "But if you're happy sharing desserts—"

"She's not ready," Josh snapped. "She's been through a lot . . . not that it's any of your damn business."

Katie set the spatula in the bowl and pushed it away. "It's not," she said. "But Josh, maybe you should take a step back and consider the fact that whatever happened to her won't fade into the background."

Yeah, he'd thought about that. And he'd questioned his sanity pursuing a woman who might never be ready to move on with her life.

"A while back," Brody said, "you said you wanted to settle down. But you've honed in on this one woman . . ." He shook his head and turned to the coffeepot.

"You haven't even brought her over for dinner," Katie said. "I've only met her at the bar."

"I think that was a good decision on my part," Josh said. "You'd interrogate her and probably scare her off."

Plus, she'd be terrified that one of you would ask too many questions.

"But Josh, you have to admit, the pies aren't working," Chad said. "You need a new strategy to win her over."

"Why don't you bring her flowers?" his sister suggested. "Or a baby goat? We have three that are just weaned. You could stop by the barn and pick one out. They're so cute."

Josh stared around the kitchen at his brothers and sister. He wanted what they had—futures filled with love and family. (Although he'd probably bypass the barn full of rescue animals on a piece of land adjoining his family homestead.)

But he was done playing games. He'd been up front and honest with Caroline. They talked over pie. He knew about her past. Or at least enough about what she'd been through to know she needed time. But more than that, he'd gotten to know *her*.

She liked ice cream with apple pie. Her humor tended toward dry and sarcastic—which matched his. And she shared his fascination for how things worked—everything from her dishwasher to the mechanical harvester he operated when cutting down trees.

"One of the things I like about Caroline," he told his siblings as he headed for the back door. "She's not playing some weird game, waiting for me to bring her flowers or, shit, a *baby goat*. Pregnancy is messing with your mind if that's your dating advice, Katie. Now, I'm going to take a shower."

He stormed out of the kitchen. But paused on the back steps and called over his shoulder: "And don't touch my pie!"

Walking to his space over the barn, he couldn't escape the feeling that his brothers and sister might be right. Not about the damn goat or his plan for trying to date her. Still, he wanted to settle down. And instead of dating, he'd spent the past year baking for a woman struggling to get her life back on track. He knew for a fact that life offered second chances, but Caroline seemed too afraid to take hers.

Maybe it was time that he stopped waiting for her to make the next move. Maybe he should ask her out.

Today.

Over key lime pie.

CAROLINE HEARD THE engine rev before the motorcycle turned the corner of the two-lane country road leading into town. And she ran for the bushes. Ducking low in the underbrush, she waited for the bike to fly by her.

Not a cop.

The Forever, Oregon, police force wasn't large. And only a few of the officers rode motorcycles. But still, she had to be careful. Although watching her back, refusing to borrow her boss's car for fear of getting pulled over, led to long walks from her borrowed room in Noah's childhood home just outside of town to her job at Big Buck's Bar—on the opposite side of downtown Forever.

Sometimes Noah's dad gave her a ride to town. And once in a while, her boss stopped by to pick her up. But the house was out of his way now that Noah and Josie had a place of their own.

And if Caroline had any hope of getting her life back on track, of moving on, then she probably needed to stop hiding in the bushes every time a car came down the road.

She dusted off her blue jeans and climbed out of the brush. Back on the shoulder of the road—she wouldn't hit sidewalks until she reached the university on the outskirts of Forever—she started walking with her backpack slung over one shoulder.

Another car came around the corner and she dove for the trees. But this time she wasn't fast enough. The vehicle slowed to a stop in the middle of the road. And her stomach turned over as dread put her nerves on high alert.

But one look and her panic eased. She knew that truck and she recognized the woman leaning out the window, her long blond hair whipping across her face.

"Caroline," Lily Greene called out. "Want a ride?"

She glanced at the blue pickup, which belonged to Lily's boyfriend, Dominic Fairmore. On any other Saturday, she would have climbed into the truck. Lily—a Forever, Oregon, native, kindergarten teacher extraordinaire, and for a few weeks most Big Buck's patrons would rather forget, bartender—knew Caroline's secrets. And

Lily still grappled with her own set of fears, though she now faced them with Dominic by her side.

But today Dominic wasn't riding shotgun. Caroline didn't recognize the man in the passenger seat. She knew the uniform though—air force dress blues.

"I can walk—"

"Ryan won't mind making room," Lily said as she guided the truck over the shoulder on the opposite side of the road.

"But you're headed out of town," she protested again. Lily might trust the man in uniform, but Caroline couldn't take that risk.

"We'll drop Ryan at his parents' place first and then I'll take you to Big Buck's. I'm guessing you have plenty of time before you need to be at work." Lily nodded to the passenger door. "Come climb in."

Lily Greene, I'm never sharing a plate of Josh's brownies with you again.

Lily knew damn well she had plenty of time. She'd planned to walk to work. "Lil, I don't want to take you out of your way. And I need to get in early. I fell behind on the dishes last night," she lied.

"Then we'll turn around and drop you first," Lily said. "It's a lot faster by car than on foot."

Caroline couldn't think of another reason not to accept the ride. If she kept protesting, Mr. Air Force would start asking questions.

"Fine." Caroline looked left, then right, and crossed the street. When she reached the other side, she found Lily's passenger standing beside the open door.

Maybe Lily had been right to dismiss Caroline's concerns. This man looked like he'd walked off a movie set with his chiseled jaw and perfect brown hair.

But then her gaze swept over the line of medals on his chest. Those were real and she doubted this smiling God among men had swiped them from an air force officer to complete his costume.

"I'm Ryan," he said, holding out his hand. "Old friend of Lily's."

"He's one of the original three musketeers," Lily called from inside the truck. "Dominic and Noah's best friend from grade school. He played football with them."

Caroline glanced over her shoulder at the man holding the door for her. Football? He was pretty, but he didn't exactly have Noah or Dominic's imposing build.

"I was the kicker," Ryan explained as he climbed up behind her. "I left to join the military when they did. But while Noah went to the Marines and Dominic to the army, I made the right call, seeing as I'm the only one still serving, and settled on the air force."

"Dominic would still be a ranger if he hadn't been injured," Lily pointed out.

"True," Ryan said. "But I think he's better off here with you."

The front bench in Dominic's pickup could technically hold three people. Still, it was a tight fit. Caroline felt Ryan's hand brush against her leg as he buckled his seat belt. But after that, he shifted toward the door. No physical contact. But he was giving her a curious look.

"So what brought you—"

"Ryan's back in town for Noah and Josie's wedding," Lily cut in as she executed an illegal U-turn. She glanced across the crowded cab as she drove them back toward downtown. "I went and picked him up at the airport so that he could surprise his parents. He didn't tell them that he's taking a full two weeks off. Isn't that sweet?

"And now when does Helena get in?" Lily continued without waiting for an answer to her first question. And Caroline decided to reconsider her brownie ban. Her friend clearly didn't plan to let Ryan guide the conversation.

"I don't know if Helena is going to make it," he said.

"What?" Lily's eyes widened, but she kept her focus on the road. "First she runs off and gets married without inviting any of her friends from home and now she won't even come back for Noah's wedding?"

He shook his head. "I don't know what's going on with her. Last time I talked to her she didn't sound like herself. I told her I'd be around for two weeks this time. I even said I could swing down to California and visit her. But she quickly told me that her husband wouldn't like it."

"He's jealous," Lily said.

"Of what?" Ryan grumbled. "I was her friend."

"Hmm," Lily murmured as she sped past the university. "Maybe I'll give her a call and try to convince her to visit. I ran into her mother at the bank. And she said Helena sends regular checks to help with the farm, but she never visits."

Lily turned to her. "Helena's mom raises Highland cattle. The meat is good and sells well. But she's had a few streaks of bad luck. Sick cows . . ."

Caroline let Lily's monologue drift over her. Familiar landmarks ticked by outside the window. A few more blocks and they would be at the bar. And free from an air force officer who had questions she couldn't answer.

Although if she planned to attend Noah's wedding, she would have to come up with something to say if anyone asked how she knew the bride and groom. And she suspected *the groom stood by me when he found out I was being raped by our commanding officer* would only lead to more questions.

But she couldn't skip Noah's wedding. He'd tried to protect her while they were deployed together. He'd found the number for the hotline when she'd given up hope of lodging a formal complaint against their commanding officer. And then, after they returned, once she'd pressed charges, Noah had testified on her behalf. He'd sworn under oath in a military court that she was telling the truth about their commanding officer. He'd risked his military career for her, though they both knew he wanted out when his term of service ended.

Nearly two years had passed since then, but she would never forget. All those nights on the base in Afghanistan when he'd gotten up and escorted her to the bathroom so that their CO wouldn't find her alone . . .

Noah had done everything he could to protect her. So one week from today, she would put on a dress and face her fears. After all, she couldn't hide forever. At some point, she had to reclaim her life—or at least pieces of it.

Lily pulled into the Big Buck's staff parking lot. "Looks like you have a visitor, Caroline."

She jumped. And she was pretty sure Ryan hadn't missed her reaction.

"Josh Summers decided to bring you another pie," Lily added. "Will you save me a piece?"

"Sure," she said. "And thanks for the ride."

Ryan climbed down from the truck and held the door open for her. "Nice meeting you. And if you see Noah, will you tell him I'll swing by the bar later?"

She nodded as she shouldered her backpack and headed for Josh. With each step, the tension eased. She'd survived a car ride with an air force officer. That had to be a step in the right direction.

"How long have you been waiting?" she asked Josh.

"Just got here," he said. "I wanted to stop by and ask you something."

Her heart sank. He'd driven over an hour out of his way to ask her out. Of course, he'd brought a pie too. But he always brought pie. And she'd known it was only a matter of time before he stopped waiting for her to name a time and place for their first date.

A month or so ago, she'd asked him out when the memory of their first kiss still pushed her past fear and landed her in a big old pile of lust-inspired insanity. She'd felt brave, bold, and maybe a little brazen.

But today she felt as if she were dodging one bullet after another. As if her life was a series of obstacles, and at the end of the day her reward was survival.

"Ask me what?" she said as she withdrew the key to the bar's back entrance from her pocket.

"Do you like whipped cream?"

She turned away from the door and faced the redhead with the sexy smile. Maybe she'd dodged enough bullets today. Maybe she could pack her concerns about the wedding, and how she planned to blend in with the flower arrangements, away until after he left.

"I love it."

"No," she said. Her tongue darted out from between her pink lips that always looked as if she was wearing a kiss-me-now lipstick. Or course, he knew the woman whose ideas of accessorizing involved a concealed weapon tucked into the waistband of her pants did not bother with makeup. She licked the whipped cream teasing the edge of her mouth. "I've got it under control."

He nodded, refilled his fork and lifted another bite of key lime pie to his mouth. He always asked—for a touch, a taste, a kiss—but he never pushed. Caroline would shift the parameters of their dessert-based friendship in her own time. Or she wouldn't and he'd be forced to come to terms with the fact that the future he daydreamed about—settling down with Caroline, buying his own home, maybe a dog—would replace sleeping with Megan Fox on the top of his Never Going to Happen list.

"You're going to Noah's wedding on Saturday night?" he asked, sliding back into friendly chitchat. He'd waited a year to kiss Caroline the first time. And he'd sit tight for another if it meant more sugarcoated kisses. To hell with his siblings' opinions.

"Just because I can take the dishwasher apart and fix it every time it tries to quit on us"—she nodded to the restaurant-grade appliance behind her—"doesn't mean Noah wouldn't fire me for missing his wedding. Plus, he's closing the bar for the night. Everyone else is going."

"Everyone else is in the wedding," Josh pointed out. Big Buck's owner and manager was marrying Forever's former bad girl, who'd burst into his life over a year ago, demanded a job, and quickly worked her way up to assistant manager. And the only other bartender on the pay-roll right now was the groom's best friend and the bride's big brother.

"True. But I owe Noah. I can't miss his wedding."

Fair enough, he thought.

"A couple of months ago, you asked me out on a date," Josh pointed out.

"I was feeling brave at the time."

"Are you canceling?" he challenged. If she said yes, he'd kiss her again. Maybe not today, but one day soon. And he'd reminder her why she'd summoned the courage to ask in the first place. He'd caught her looking, her eyes roaming over his biceps with a flicker of something more than friendship in their green depths. And if given the chance, he would let her run her fingers over his T-shirt, mapping the muscles beneath . . .

"No, I'm not canceling," she said thoughtfully. "I'm still working out the details."

"Be my date to the wedding."

Her eyes widened, staring back at him as if he'd dropped to one knee and suggested they follow her boss down the aisle.

"No," she said firmly. "Josh, I . . . Just no."

CAROLINE REFUSED TO look away. She'd spent months learning to read Josh's facial expressions, forcing herself to look past the red-gold stubble that screamed 'I'm too sexy for this bar.'

Or his shirt.

Or her . . .

Right now, the corners of his mouth threatened to fall into a frown. Disappointment. But he never let his smile falter for long. He always took a moment. Looked away and then returned his gaze to her as if she hadn't turned him down twice in ten minutes.

But he knows I'm a long way from whipped cream kisses in the bar's back room.

And dates.

Yes, she'd asked him out once. But then reality had come crashing down on her. Her life consisted of washing pint glasses and staying out of sight. She couldn't hope for more—not even a single night out at one of the restaurants near the university—with a federal warrant hanging over her head.

Of course, the police weren't actively looking for her. As far as she knew. But if the local cops, or even a state trooper passing through town, found out who she was . . . If they learned why she kept to the shadows, she would be under arrest and turned over to the military. She would have to pay the price for her unauthorized absence. For refusing to deploy alongside the men who'd turned a blind eye when their commanding officer ordered her into his bed. The men who'd laughed with Dustin when he'd said he would force open her mouth and make her take him between her lips . . .

And then there was the elephant in the bar's back room that would also tag along on their date. She hadn't had sex—oral or otherwise—because *she* wanted to since before she joined the Marines. Josh had never treated her like a victim, but there was a first time for everything.

"I'm sorry," she added. "But I can't go to the wedding as your date. There will be too many people. And everyone knows you. If they see me with you . . . they'll ask questions. And I can't give them answers. I need to stay in the background, hiding behind a plant or something. And then leave as soon as they cut the cake."

"A wedding probably isn't the best place for a first date." He pointed his fork at her. "Maybe once I get my own place, you can help me christen the kitchen."

She raised an eyebrow. "That assumes a lot for a first date."

He laughed. And the familiar sound threatened to lead her into his version of the future. One where they would kiss in the kitchen and then—

"I was talking about baking a pie together," he said. "I'd invite you over to the farmhouse, but I didn't think you'd take kindly to receiving the third degree from my siblings and their significant others."

"Probably not a good idea," she murmured. She'd spent the past year trying to avoid his two older brothers and his sister. It wasn't hard seeing as his family lived in Independence Falls, a solid hour's drive from Big Buck's Bar. Chad Summers, the middle brother, had tried to befriend her, stopping by the bar's back room with his girlfriend, a drop-dead gorgeous woman who'd served in the army. But Caroline had shut down their attempts.

Josh Summers remained the one and only person she'd let in since she'd showed up on Noah's doorstep.

There was something about the way he accepted the word 'no' that broke down her defenses. He never tossed the word aside, questioning whether it was a knee-jerk response. He never pushed—not once—under the pretense that he knew what was best for her. Not since that first night when he'd found her in the woods. Even Noah, who'd had her back when they were deployed together, pushed. Her fellow soldier turned boss tried over and over to talk her into visiting the local gun club with him. She said no and he asked again and again.

But Josh always listened.

"Have you started looking for a new apartment?" she asked, steering the conversation away from dates that might lead to compromising situations.

"I'm looking, but not for an apartment. I'm still sitting on my split from when we sold the family trucking company. I want to use the cash to buy a piece of land. Someplace with a nice view of the mountains, maybe space to put those viticulture classes I've been taking to use and grow some grapes. Not a lot. I've learned enough to know that is one tough business. I'd rather keep my day job with Moore Timber and put my blood, sweat, and tears into building my own home."

"You can do that?" The question slipped out before she could mask the surprise in her voice.

"I'll need help, but I know what I want. Four bedrooms. Maybe five. Plenty of space to spread out. Timber frame. A second story that is open to a great room below. And one helluva kitchen with all the modern appliances.

I'll hire an architect, and a builder. But I can swing a hammer with the best of them."

Four bedrooms. Plenty of space. . .

Oh hell, she should push him away. A better friend would demand that Josh Summers share his pies with a woman willing to daydream about a place in his picture-perfect future. She shouldn't let him waste his life waiting for her to make up her mind about a first date.

"You should do it," she said firmly. "You should buy the land. What are you waiting for?"

He cocked his head. One red curl fell across his forehead. His hair looked as if he'd rolled out of bed, run his fingers through the loose, wavy locks and prepared to face another day looking like an Irish god who'd somehow landed in rural Oregon. Though that might have something to do with the muscles he'd fine-tuned over the years of felling trees.

But right now she kept her gaze focused on his face, waiting for his answer.

"What if I decide on five bedrooms and the woman I want to share my dream home with thinks it's too much. I might have to settle for three in order to talk her into an outdoor kitchen that I'm thinking about building in addition to the monstrous one in the house."

"As long as you're not planning to turn half the house into some sort of man cave with beer pong tables lining the hallways, I think you'll find someone who will love your dream house," she said. "Of course to meet that special someone you will have to start dating."

And that was as close as she was going to get to kicking him in the butt and demanding that he turn his focus away from her. They could remain friends. But another kiss would just lead to a dead end.

His smile faded. "You think I should ask someone else to be my date to the wedding?"

She forced a brief nod and let her gaze settle on the half-eaten pie.

"No," he said slowly, lingering over the simple word. "I don't think so. But I might put in an offer on that land."

"You should do both," she pointed out despite the relief that threatened to turn to joy. "I can't move into your four- to five-bedroom dream home. Not when I'm still so . . ."

Scared.

Nearly fifteen months had slipped by since she'd run away from the military. She'd pressed pause on her life that day. There had been moments here and there were she'd felt ready to hit play again and move on. Each one revolved around the man standing across the stainless steel counter looking down at his pie.

"A couple of weeks ago you stopped wearing those baggy cargo pants." Josh dug his fork into the dish and glanced up at her. "I like the skinny jeans better."

Me too. And I like the way you look at my legs when you think I'm distracted. . .

"I stood out in the cargo pants and boots," she said with a shrug. "Lily said I'd blend in more if I dressed like the university students. And Josie had some clothes she didn't think would ever fit again even if she lost all the baby weight. She gave these to me."

"You stand out in those jeans too. I'm glad I only have to share the view with the dishwasher." He nodded to the machine. "And not all those young kids from the college."

"You're twenty-eight, Josh. Not that much older than those 'young kids.' Many of them are graduate students."

"More than half would love to have you serve their drinks," he said.

"I like it back here where no one will—"

"Notice you. Yeah, I get that. But my point is, you've changed since you first showed up here looking for Noah." He set down his fork and took a step back. "Who knows what will happen next?"

"Nothing."

I hope. I pray.

Because the only life-changing events she could imagine would land her in trouble. She'd carved out a safe place to hide. She had a cash job and a place to live thanks to her boss. If she lost this—

"Something always happens next." He turned and headed for the door.

She'd touched the hard planes of his chest when she'd kissed him, but the view of his backside left her wanting more. More pies. More conversation. More Josh.

One . . . Two . . . Three. . .

He turned and glanced over his shoulder. And then he flashed a knowing smile. Oh, she'd seen plenty of hard-bodied men. She'd served alongside soldiers with drool-worthy muscles. There was nothing special about Josh Summers.

Except for his smile.

She was falling for that grin and the man who wielded it like an enticing treat. Tempted to trust in him. Believe in him.

"I'll see you at the wedding," he called and then he walked his delicious smile out the door of the bar's back room.

She abandoned her fork and dipped her fingers in the pie dish. Sugar. She needed a burst of sweetness to take her mind off Josh Summers.

Next time he asks you to lick the whipped cream from your lips, say yes!

Because Josh Summers was right. Something always happened next. And if she wanted to reclaim her life—or at least a small piece of it—if she wished for another chance to land in Josh's arms with his lips pressed to hers, then she needed to find out what happened when she said yes.

Chapter 3

"I BET YOU'RE wondering the same thing I am."

"I doubt that, Miss Lily." Josh lowered his plastic pint glass from his lips, savoring the taste of the state's leading microbrew, which Josie Fairmore—now Mrs. Josephine Tager—had declared the signature drink for her backyard wedding. "But if you're mentally undressing other women at parties you should probably tell Dominic. Trust me, that is something your boyfriend would want to know."

Lily Greene stepped in front of him. Long blond hair cascaded over her shoulders, teasing the neckline of her strapless pink dress, but Josh didn't give a damn about the curves beneath the bubble-gum colored fabric. She was blocking his view of the only woman he wanted to see naked.

Caroline.

"I've never seen Caroline in a dress," Lily mused. "Where does she keep her gun under that outfit?"

"If I talk her out of it later, I'll let you know." He tried to step around Lily. He'd kept his distance from Caroline during the ceremony, but now that the reception was in full swing under the rented tent beside Noah's old barn, he wanted to talk to the woman who'd walked in here looking like she'd borrowed a page from his fantasies.

Tight dress, high heels, no panties. . .

OK, he couldn't say for sure she'd skipped the underwear from this vantage point. But he could see her pale green sundress. The top hugged her torso. He'd felt her full breasts when Caroline pressed up against him during the one and only time they'd kissed. And yeah, he'd been surprised by how much she'd been hiding behind those baggy shirts she wore to Big Buck's.

She'd filled out since the first night he found her in the woods looking like she hadn't eaten much while freaking *walking* from Northern California. But she was still petite, even in those high-heeled wedges strapped to her feet.

The bride of the hour had once described Caroline's look as 'wood nymph meets G.I. Jane' when someone suggested they looked alike. And Josh had to agree. Josie and Caroline were roughly the same height, similar dark hair and pale skin, but the similarities stopped there. There was something about the way Caroline carried herself—a little wild and rough around the edges—that set her apart.

He cocked his head and studied Caroline's slim ankles and muscular calves. How had he known this woman for over a year and never seen her legs? And while he was asking questions, he couldn't escape the one his brothers hurled at him over and over: how long did he plan to wait for her? As his big brother had kindly pointed out last week, Josh hadn't slept with a woman since before he first met Caroline.

But he'd learned patience since his accident. Losing his short-term memory, spending months in rehab, working his ass off to reclaim his sense of self, he'd grown accustomed to waiting for what he wanted.

Still, he'd like to find out if Caroline had attended the wedding without her panties.

Lily reached out and took his free hand. "I think she needs a friend tonight. She's still afraid of Ryan. And probably most of the other unfamiliar faces. There are a lot of cops here."

"I know." He pulled free from Lily's hold and stepped around her. Then he walked around the wooden dance floor Noah had installed for the reception. He waved to friends and familiar faces that called his name, but he kept his gaze focused on Caroline. The closer he got the more the dress looked like a disguise—an attempt to soften her don't-mess-with-me façade

She'd planted her high-heeled wedges hip's distance apart. And her hands were clasped behind her back. Parade rest. He recognized the stance. It was as if her military training had seeped into her bones, becoming a permanent part of her. Caroline was a Marine.

A Marine driven into fucking hiding.

Not a lot pissed Josh off. He let go of most of the shit life hurled at him. He'd come too close to losing his chance to live to hold on tight to anger. But he wanted five minutes alone with the man who'd stolen away her future with the military. He wouldn't bring a weapon, just his fists and his rage.

But Caroline didn't need him to seek out vengeance on her behalf. She didn't need a hero. Hell, she *was* a hero. Lily had nailed it—the fierce, frightened Marine needed a friend. Especially tonight.

He kept walking, setting his empty drink on the makeshift bar as he passed by. He grinned at Dominic Fairmore. "Might want to hand over your self-appointed role as master of the keg to someone else. Your girlfriend is mentally undressing other women."

"What the—"

Josh just laughed and kept walking. His target had shifted back a step, or hell, ten. She looked as if she was on the verge of ditching the reception before they cut the cake. But then she resumed her go-to stance with her fingers touching the tent flaps.

If she wants to blend in, she needs to stop posing like she's the freaking hired security, ready to kick some ass...

When Josh first heard her story, he'd wondered if he'd stumbled on the right Caroline in the woods. The woman he'd mistaken for a protesting environmentalist was a fighter. Sure, Noah had spent the past year reminding Josh that her shitastic history labeled her a 'victim' and Josh had pretended to listen. But he didn't see it.

If he had to describe the woman trying to blend into the side of the white rental tent, he'd toss out strong, sexy, and likely to pull a gun on him.

And shit, it looked like he wasn't the only one who thought so—about the gun part at least. The man who ran Forever's police department when he wasn't playing the part of father of the bride stood in front of Caroline. Josh could see the question in the police chief's gaze from ten paces away and fought the urge to run to her side.

"There you are." Caroline took his hand and pulled him to her. "You slipped away to grab drinks and came back empty-handed?"

"I ran into a few people." He nodded to Chief Fairmore. "Congratulations. Your daughter was the happiest bride I've ever witnessed. And I've seen quite a few now that all my siblings are settling down."

The police chief beamed. "I take it you're next in line."

That's the plan, but I fell for a woman who's hiding from, well, you.

"I came over to welcome the one stranger in the crowd," Chief Fairmore continued. "And learned she was your date for the evening."

Josh nodded and tried to make sense of the web of lies Caroline had spun for the bride's curious father. As a rule, Josh stuck to the truth. It was the one lesson his late father had drilled into him over and over. No matter what kind of trouble he landed in as a kid, he had to fess up.

Caroline squeezed his hand. "I told him how we met at the bar when I started working there."

"Josie mentioned they'd hired a dishwasher," the police chief said, his curiosity still honed in on Caroline. "What brought you to Forever? The university?"

Caroline's nails dug into his hand. He knew she was

about his age, but could easily pass for younger—maybe twenty-three, twenty-four, around the same age as the glowing bride.

"No, I was just passing through," she said, her voice wavering slightly. "Then I met Josh—"

"I asked her to give Forever a chance. Why head to Portland when you can live and work here? I mean this town is amazing, right?" Josh said, jumping into her lie and adding to the story. He had a feeling she'd been vague. No mention of her previous connection to Noah or the military. But people in Forever were born curious, especially the man paid to keep the peace and follow the law.

Caroline nodded and forced a smile. "He was very convincing."

"We're glad to have you," Chief Fairmore said. "And I know my daughter is happy to have your help at the bar. She tells me business is booming over there. Judging from the number of underage college kids trying to slip past the bouncers, I know she's telling the truth."

"She is. Now, if you'll excuse us, Chief, I owe my girl a drink." Josh drew her close and snaked his arm around her slim waist. He wanted to get her away from the father of the bride before she started talking about how much she loved washing the piles of pint glasses at the bar.

Plus there's a chance she left her panties at home but strapped her gun to her thigh.

"Good to see you." The police chief held out his right hand and Josh gave it a firm shake. "Give my best to your family."

"Will do, sir," he said as he led Caroline away.

The side of her body pressed against him as they moved. Tension pulsed through her, leading to hurried steps, and he wondered what would happen if he released her.

She would run.

"Thirsty?" he murmured, keeping a tight hold on her.

She ignored the question. He caught her gaze darting to the exit. "If I leave now—without you—he'll be suspicious."

"Stay with me," he said.

But not just to fool the chief of police.

Yeah, he better keep that to himself until they could talk without a tent full of onlookers.

"I'll get you that drink," he added.

"I'm fine." She slowed her frantic pace as they approached the makeshift bar. Then she drew to a halt ten paces from the bar where Dominic stood chatting with the woman of the hour in the flowing white gown. Caroline tilted her chin up until her gaze met his. Her kiss-me pink lips formed a thin line. "But I owe you—"

He shook his head. "No, you don't, Caroline."

He wanted Caroline—in his life, in his bed, and in his dream home. He wanted to turn her lies into the real deal, but not because she owed him.

Sure, he'd lied for her. And he'd do it again in a heartbeat. He would never leave her open to unwanted questions. All because she'd summoned the freaking courage to put on a dress and slip out of her routine for one night. She'd taken so many hits, each one knocking her further and further off track, messing with her mind and heaping fears onto a woman who'd already suffered too much.

He wanted to be there if the train derailed. She was strong. So damn strong. But life didn't play fair. He knew that better than anyone.

He'd endured his share of hits. But he'd always gotten back up and waited for the next one, determined to take another shot at finding the special formula that led to the kind of happiness that stood strong through life's ups and downs. His brothers and sister had found it. He knew it was out there.

"You don't owe me anything," he said firmly.

"Thank you," she murmured, the words barely above a whisper.

Keep your gratitude. I want you. Just you.

He wanted to hold her, talk to her, kiss her . . . And if now wasn't the time or the place, hell, he'd find another.

He drew Caroline in front of him. Placing his hands on her waist, careful to keep his touch light, he looked down into her green eyes. "Do you trust me?"

"As much as I trust anyone," she said.

She didn't say no.

The smile hit him hard and fast even though he knew her answer was a far cry from yes. Grinning like he'd won the freaking lottery, he released her right hip and raised his hand to her mouth. He ran his thumb over the pad of her lips and murmured, "Kiss me. Long and hard."

Her brow knit together. "And that will tell Josie's dad and the rest of the police force—"

"That we're sharing a helluva lot more than pies. But

don't do it for them. Kiss me because you want to. Because you remember what if felt like last time and you want—"

"More." She raised her hands to his face and cupped his jaw. Her gaze honed in on his lips as if assessing her target. Then she rose up on her toes and leaned forward. Her lips brushed his and he closed his eyes. The reception faded into the background. Music, voices, the sounds of laughter and joy blended together.

Don't pull back.

He tightened his hold on her hips. If she refused to deepen the kiss, he'd settle for long. They'd work their way up to hard.

Already there. . .

But his hard-on wasn't invited to this kiss.

Caroline stepped forward and pressed her body against his. Her lips parted as their gentle kiss shifted into hot-and-heavy territory. Their tongues touched. Greedy. Hungry. And oh man, he felt a surge of desire to take everything this woman had to give.

She moved closer until she practically straddled his left leg. His fingers dug into the fabric of her dress. His hands were tempted to roam over her lower back, to search for a sign that she'd forgotten her underwear, but he kept the impulse in check. Her inner thigh brushed his.

No gun.

Stripped of her defenses—her weapon, her don't-mess-with-me baggy T-shirt, and her place in the shadows—Caroline was a bold, passionate woman. And he hated the fact that labels held her back. *Victim. Outlaw.* She was so much more than her past.

She released her hold on him and broke the kiss.

"Now what?" she murmured.

He caught her hand in his. "Now we take a walk."

"Josh—"

"We need to talk." He led her past the dance floor and through the maze of tables. He nodded to Noah, who was staring after them, probably debating if he should step in and demand to know what the hell was going on. But Caroline had told her friend to stay out of her 'friendship' with Josh. And the groom trusted her to take care of herself—most of the time.

They stepped out of the tent and headed into the night. Stars blanketed the sky overhead and a nearly full moon illuminated the grassy stretch between the reception and the old barn. Josh debated checking the door to see if the groom had locked it up for the party. The old building was home to a handful of cats and the old mechanical bull from Big Buck's days as a country western barn catering to loggers instead of college kids.

He glanced at Caroline. "Cold?"

"I'm fine." She stopped and pulled her hand free from his grip. "It's warm still. Especially for September."

"Yeah. Dry too."

"Why are we out here, Josh?" she demanded, crossing her arms in front of her chest. Heck, she looked badass even in the pale green sundress with her lips red from their kiss.

"I want you. So damn much. And you sure as hell haven't missed that fact."

"No." Her gaze drifted to his fly as if recalling the feel of his erection pressed against her. "You've dropped off a lot of pies."

He nodded. "I like baking for you. And I swear I will lie to keep you safe if I need to. But I want more."

"More," she repeated.

He nodded, knowing his next question would probably earn him a big fat no. But she'd kissed him with a hunger that matched his own. She'd turned to him for help when the chief of police questioned her. "So what do you say? How about we give dating a shot?"

CAROLINE FOUGHT THE urge to move away from the man who'd broken through her barriers. Tilting her head back, she stared up at the stars. He'd found her under the night sky over a year ago. And she'd known better than to put her faith in him then.

But she'd let him draw her away from the grip of isolation. She'd let down her guard. She allowed the feeling that someone—the military, the police, or her rapist—was hunting her to slip away when she was with him. Josh had taken the time to get to know her, slow and steady as if he had all the time in the world.

That time had just run out.

"And if I say no?"

"Then the answer is no, Caroline."

She studied the constellations, picking out the few she'd learned as a child. These same stars had followed her around the world, unchanged by the events that had uprooted her life.

But everything on earth moved forward. When she'd first run away, she'd felt as if she had more in common with the stars. Her future felt stagnant, reduced to hiding, running, and more hiding.

By lying to the police chief, she'd tried to drag Josh into hiding with her. Part of her admired him for being brave enough to say no to perpetuating an illusion. He could have tried to win her over under the cover of deception. But he wouldn't do that.

"You asked me out before," he said. "And yeah, you have every reason, every right to change your mind."

She lowered her chin and looked him straight in the eyes. She waited for his too-charming smile. But his lips formed a thin line.

"We could start with dinner," he continued. "Someplace you're comfortable. In town. Or someplace where nobody knows us. I'll drive you up to Portland on your next night off if you want."

She found herself nodding. Dinner. Someplace safe. They would be an ordinary couple.

"And no sex," he added. "I promise."

The words felt like a direct hit and her defenses rose up. "Without the possibility of sex," she said, "we're just two friends sharing a meal."

"Caroline—"

"Sex stays on the table." She unfolded her arms and allowed them to drift down to her sides. She fought the urge to clasp them behind her back and assume a parade rest position. She was moving on, moving forward toward a future that glowed bright despite the past. "I'm not saying we'll head back to your place or mine tonight—"

"You live here." He nodded to the farmhouse separated from the barn by a gravel parking area. "With Noah's dad."

"I'm not saying it will happen on the first date," she continued, summoning the courage that had thrust her into his arms for that first kiss in the back room at Big Buck's and again tonight. "And we don't need to choose between my place or yours. I grew up with an overprotective mom. Once upon a time, I knew how to make the most of the limited space in the backseat of a car. And your pickup has a lot more room in the front."

He cocked his head. "I don't know. With the stick and all, it might be tricky."

"It might." She stepped away before she moved into his arms. She'd ridden a roller coaster of emotions tonight. At the top, she'd faced possible discovery by the police. Fear had swept her down and somehow landed her back in 'once upon a time.'

"I guess we'll find out." She sidestepped and walked past Josh, heading for the tent. "Not on the first date," she added, her voice soft and low. "But maybe by the third. Or perhaps the tenth . . ."

"Caroline." He reached out and ran his fingertips over her bare arm. But he stopped short of grabbing ahold of her and pulling her to him. "If we wait until the tenth date, I promise I'll have mapped out a way to work around the stick shift."

Chapter 4

WHAT DO I wear to a date when I hope to end the night making out in the front seat of a truck?

Caroline scanned her meager wardrobe. She'd filled Noah's guest room closet with a line of Big Buck's T-shirts, three pairs of hand-me-down jeans from Josie, two pairs of faded black cargo pants, and the green sundress she'd worn to the wedding. She'd left every other piece of clothing that she owned behind in California when she'd run away. Her older sister's attic held boxes of cute tops and fun, flirty dresses from her life before she'd joined the Marines. But she'd enlisted at nineteen and she doubted those nine-year-old clothes would be in style even if she had access to them.

She closed the closet door and headed to the landline in the kitchen. A cell phone still felt like a risk. It was too easy for the authorities to track if they were still looking for her. And a cell was an unnecessary expense considering she couldn't afford new clothes. She picked up the receiver and dialed the bar. It was ten in the morning on a Monday, only two days after his wedding, but she knew Noah would be at Big Buck's.

The happy couple had put their honeymoon on hold until their daughter was a little older. At eleven months old, little Isabelle was still nursing. Plus, Josie wanted to pay down her debt from the heartbreaking past that had sent her running home to Forever—and landed her in Noah's arms—before they planned a trip.

"Big Buck's Bar. This is—"

"Noah," Caroline cut in. "I need to borrow Josie for a few hours. Is she around?"

"She's in the back. Everything all right?"

Caroline heard footsteps as her friend and boss moved through the bar, heading to the room that held the dishwasher. "I need help putting together an outfit for tonight."

"Where are you going?" he demanded.

"Out." The man who'd appointed himself her honorary big brother did not need details.

"Where?"

She stared out the window at the barn. One of Noah's rescue cats stalked across the gravel as if preparing to pounce. Caroline had a feeling there would be a dead bird or mouse waiting on the porch when she returned home from her date.

"Caroline?" Noah said.

He'll find out from Josie or Lily. Someone would clue him in to the fact that she was officially dating Josh Summers.

He might even hear it from his new father-in-law. And then, Noah would come to her with a pile of questions.

"Josh is taking me out to dinner."

And cue the crickets . . .

The footsteps on the other end of the line stopped. She could hear Noah breathing as he struggled to hold back a *what the hell, Caroline?*

"Did he coerce you?" Noah enunciated each word, his tone low and ominous. "I heard about what happened at the party. You had a run-in with Josie's dad—"

"I want to go out with him," she blurted. "I'm tired of hiding. I go to the bar. I come back here. Once or twice I've stopped by Lily's house. I'm ready to get out there . . . but I don't have anything to wear. I need shoes. Something soft and feminine. I can't wear combat boots. What kind of message does that send?"

"I'll kick your ass if you get fresh with me?" Noah murmured.

"I could, but I don't think attacking my date is the best way to get him on his back."

"Caroline—"

"I was good at this once," she said firmly. "You didn't know me then. Before we deployed together. But back then I went out on dates. I flirted."

I wasn't afraid.

She heard the familiar whoosh through the phone as Noah pushed open the swinging door that led to the bar's back room.

"Josie," he called. "You're needed at my dad's place. Caroline is having a shoe crisis."

CAROLINE PACED THE kitchen and fought the urge to unlock the gun safe. She'd talked Noah's dad into giving her the combination months ago. Sometimes she needed the added comfort of a loaded weapon against her leg. Logic suggested that her rapist would have hunted her down by now if he still held the end of his illustrious military career against her. But logic and fear didn't always play nice together.

More than a year had passed since she last saw her former CO in the doorway to her sister's home. He'd suffered a dishonorable discharge for adultery. With Noah's testimony, the military court had accepted the fact that she had a sexual relationship with him. But she couldn't prove her CO had forced her. And oh the irony, the man who'd promised to lead her through a war zone then forcibly removed her clothes from her body, he dared to blame *her* for losing his job.

She refused to let that man hurt her again. But as the possibility of an attack slipped further and further away, her need for a gun strapped to her thigh or tucked into the waistband of her pants should have disappeared too. But the feelings still haunted her even if the man had given up.

Alone . . . Afraid . . . Skirting the edge of depression as if it were a deep pool she might stumble into . . .

But not tonight.

She circled the table, her fingers brushing the tops of the four chairs as she walked. Her fitted grey jeans and flowing, sleeveless pink blouse didn't exactly scream, 'accessorize with a handgun.' Josie had lent her the clothes along with a pair of black leather ankle boots. And if she planned to kick some ass in these shoes, she better be prepared to balance on her toes—or use the three-inch spikes attached to the back of the boots.

She heard the crunch of gravel before Josh's pickup pulled into the parking area. The cat abandoned her prey and ran for the barn. And Caroline debated following the scared animal. But she wouldn't get far in these stilts masquerading as footwear . . .

Her date stepped down from his silver pickup. He'd given his ride a bath. Even the tires sparkled in the early evening light, no traces of mud from his latest harvest site. She suspected a chainsaw and a pile of safety gear hid in the bed of his truck, but he'd covered his tools for the night.

And the owner of the shiny silver pickup had cleaned up too. He'd traded his lumberjack uniform—button-down flannel and cargo pants—for a pair of clean blue jeans and a green short-sleeve polo. The bright shirt drew her attention to his red curls. He'd stopped short of running styling gel through his hair, but he'd clearly tried to tame the curls. And then run his fingers through them a time or ten, probably on the drive over here.

They'd both gone to a lot of effort for this date. What if they got to dinner and found they had nothing to talk about? She didn't exactly have a lot to say about her current career. Most of it he'd heard before. And he'd already explained the finer points of felling trees over pie.

"Evening, Caroline," he called from the front door.

He stopped in the entryway separating the kitchen

from the hall. His shoulder rested against the wooden door frame. His gaze met hers then shifted lower to her pink shirt, down her jean-clad legs to the stupid high-heeled boots. She fought the urge to shift her weight from one foot to the other under his scrutiny.

"You look beautiful." He spoke in a low rumble as his gaze met hers again.

"I borrowed the clothes from Josie," she said.

"They look good on you."

"Thank you," she mumbled, shoving her hands in the back pockets of her jeans.

His lips curved into a smile. "Ready?"

No.

But if not now, when? She couldn't go back to the person she'd been before the Marines. She had to take a step forward.

Or stay right here paralyzed by fear. . .

She withdrew her hands and plucked her borrowed clutch from the table. Josie had claimed the worn black leather handbag matched her boots. And Caroline had agreed to carry the purse instead of her battered back-pack. Then she drew a deep breath.

"I'm ready," she confirmed.

He pushed off the door frame. "To go forth and con-quer? Or for a first date?"

"One and the same, right?" Caroline marched over to him.

Josh laughed as he led the way down the short entry hall and held the front door open for her. "All right then," he said.

She hit the gravel before him, but he quickly caught up with her. Stupid boots. The heels sunk into the rocky surface and threatened to throw her off balance. But she fought back.

"Nice shoes," he said when they reached the passenger side door. "But your combat boots might have been a better choice for tonight."

Her brow knit together. "Where are you taking me?"

Josh dialed up the charm as his lips formed another megawatt grin. The hint of stubble and the twinkle in his green eyes only added to his allure. He pulled the door open and gestured for her to climb in.

"Where—"

"Tonight I'm taking my dream girl to one of my favorite spots in the Willamette Valley. I've always wanted to take a date to this place. But it never felt right before."

She stared at him. *Dream girl? It never felt right?* There were so many things wrong with that response. And she still didn't have a clue why she should have worn combat boots.

"You'll see when we get there," he added. "If you climb into the truck."

She maneuvered into the passenger seat. By the time she'd fastened her seat belt, he'd claimed his place behind the wheel.

"Dream girl?" she said.

"Front and center in my fantasies for the past year." He put the truck in gear and headed down the drive to the main road. "Hell, I bet I have a better idea about what you look like naked than you do."

"You've never seen me naked."

"But I have a world-class imagination."

She kept her gaze focused on the road, noting the turns. She rarely drove, but she'd learned her way around the town. And she'd walked the dirt roads that skirted around downtown Forever plenty of times.

If she glanced at him, he might question the heat rising to her cheeks. He wasn't the only one with an imagination. She'd memorized the way his work jeans hugged his butt. And daydreamed about the feel of his hard chest beneath her hands.

"Good day?" he asked as they barreled down the country road kicking up dust.

"Quiet," she said. "Until Josie came by with Isabelle and half her closet. What about you?"

"Chad and I headed over to a tract of land Moore Timber's been hired to harvest. We're trying to figure out if we can get trucks in there or if we need the helicopter. The incline is pretty steep, so I'm guessing Chad will get to fly on this one."

"Do you mind working with a helicopter?" she asked.

"After one hit me on the head and tried to kill me?" He glanced over at her. "My brother wasn't flying that one, so I feel pretty safe out there now. Chad and I have gotten into it once or twice, but not much since he settled down with Lena. He has better things to do in his downtime than take a swing at me."

No flashbacks? No paranoid feelings it might happen again?

"Plus, I got my short-term memory back. No permanent damage. And it's not like I remember what happened, so pretty easy to put it behind me. The past is in the past and all that."

He turned onto a narrow dirt driveway. But she'd been too focused on his words to look for a sign out front. He'd reclaimed his memory. He'd let the past go. If only it was that simple for her. If only she could take back what had been stolen from her.

JOSH PUSHED ON the brake and slowed the truck to a stop. Then he put it in park and turned to her. The surprise, dinner—it could all wait until his date returned to the present. Right now, she was staring out the window as if her thoughts were miles away.

Something he said? He replayed their conversation over.

No permanent damage.

Yeah, her past wasn't locked away. And it had done some serious damage. He hoped like hell it wasn't permanent. The fact that she'd taken a chance on him suggested she might be ready to move forward. Sure, she'd waited a year before she'd asked. And longer before she agreed to a date and time. But she'd gone all in, dressing up for him.

He studied her outfit. The pink shirt's spaghetti straps offered one helluva view of her toned shoulders. He'd never had a thing for women's arms. Tonight, in that shirt, she might turn him into a convert. He wanted to run his hand over her smooth, bare skin. Get up close and personal with her toned biceps.

But first he needed to hit the reset button on their date. "I know it's not that easy for you," he added.

"No, it's not." Her chin dropped to her chest as if she wished to study her hands clasped tight in her lap. "I was fearless when I joined the Marines. Even after my first deployment to Afghanistan, I was shaken, but still strong. I knew it wasn't all sunshine and roses over there. I knew guys who were blown to pieces while on patrol. And I'd endured plenty of snide, sexist comments. But there were a lot of good guys too. So I signed on for another five years. I dreamed about promotions. And I thought I would be better the next time I deployed. With experience, I'd be able to do more. I was twenty-four. Older and wiser." She let out a harsh bark of laughter. "I thought I would become better. And instead . . . instead I became less."

"No," he said firmly.

"You didn't know me before," she said firmly. "I was fierce. At nineteen. At twenty-four."

"Still are," he said.

She looked up at him with those sharp eyes. Her mouth formed a thin line. She looked more intimidating than half the crew chiefs he worked with and those guys easily had fifty pounds on her.

"Do you know how many times I've checked over my shoulder today?" she demanded. "I'm scared and I can't run from the feeling. It follows me, stripping away who I was."

"You're still the toughest woman I know. And my brothers hooked up with some pretty badass chicks," he said. "But you're the most interesting. Certainly the sexiest. Although I've never pictured Kat or Lena naked. Chad would kick my ass for that. And even Brody might take a swing at me."

He won a small smile. But he'd hoped for a laugh. He leaned over, resting his right forearm on the center console. He raised his left and brushed the back of his hand over her cheek before lowering it to the car's center. "Caroline—"

"I wanted to be less of myself. After he attacked me. The way I looked. The way I behaved—I wanted to wipe it all away. It took taking a step back and coming home to the States before I woke up to the fact that he didn't attack me because of how I looked or because I tried so hard to fit in and be 'one of the guys.'"

Josh stared at his date. Suddenly the gulf between a second kiss at a wedding—under the pretense of a false relationship—and where they stood now looked like a river lined with white-water rapids instead of the smooth first date pond. What if he'd messed up and she wasn't ready to date again? What the hell did he know about surviving rape? Or shit, surviving a war? He'd never served.

But he'd had his sense of self stripped away along with his memory. And he'd been pulled close to depression waiting for it to return, wondering if he'd ever wake up with a clear picture of what had happened yesterday or the day before that.

After all of that, he'd changed too. It hadn't happened overnight, but gradually, he'd looked for a different future, ready to claim his second chance. Caroline wasn't there yet and he could respect that.

"You're right," he said. "I didn't know you before. But I know you're locked into some sort of epic battle with fear. I saw you pull a gun on that raccoon behind Big Buck's when you first moved to town. Shit, I don't mind if you're carrying tonight."

"I'm not," she said firmly.

He let his gaze shift away from her dead-serious expression. He lingered over her loose-fitting shirt. "Really? Because I've been imagining all the places you might be hiding—"

"Josh."

Her voice shifted from serious to doom-and-gloom. And he knew it was time to save his first date.

"OK, I'll be serious for a second. But after this we're going back to traditional first date chitchat. We're not on some reality dating show. I hate to break it to you, but I don't have a rose for you at the end of the night if you spill your guts and put on a good show. And . . ."

He pulled away from her and sat upright in his seat. "Wait for it now, because I'm going to be straight up honest with you right now. I like you, Caroline. You're straightforward. No games. And that works for me. I've spent the past year telling myself that if I show you respect and offer friendship, we might land right here on a date. So how about we go into the winery, grab the picnic basket they prepared for us, and hike out to one of my favorite spots in the great state of Oregon."

She cocked her head. "I thought most dates started with a rose, not ended with one."

He pushed open his door. "Do you live under a rock? There's this reality dating show—"

"I know, Josh. It was a joke." She followed his lead and climbed down from the truck. "And I promise I'll save the rest of the heavy conversation for the hot tub."

"Looks like we got lost on the way to the hot tub." Caroline added a note of mock despair to her voice.

"I must have made a wrong turn," he teased as he put the truck in park and cut the lights. The bright, nearly full moon illuminated the pickup's interior.

"I guess that means the heavy conversation will have to wait for our second date," she added. "But after hiking through grape vines in these crazy heels—"

"You took them off ten feet into the field," he said nodding to the shoes resting next to her feet.

"I'll put them back on if that will win me a steamy make-out session in the front of your truck," she said holding tight to the brave and bold feelings she'd stumbled on during their walk through the vineyard. She had revealed more about herself, how she'd felt in the aftermath of what had happened to her in Afghanistan, than she'd told anyone else, including her sister, Noah, and her parents.

Though to be fair, she knew her parents believed her former CO. Her father had served in the Marines too and he'd held tight to the 'good soldier' defense. Her mother followed her dad's lead, choosing to believe Dustin's version of events. So she'd never confided in them.

But Josh had listened and come back with the unexpected *I like who you are now*. Then he'd taken her out to a quiet, secluded spot overlooking the valley below. He'd poured her a glass of wine and told her about what he'd learned in his wine making course. And he'd made her laugh, reminding her why she'd looked forward to his visits each week.

Because he didn't look at her and see less of the person she'd been before. He just saw her.

"You know, I usually have this rule about kissing barefoot," he said. "But for you, I'll make an exception."

"An exception?"

"If—"

Her eyes widened. "There's an if?"

"*If* you take off your shirt."

"I think you've been misreading all of those 'no shirt, no shoes, no service' signs." She leaned forward, slowly closing the gap between them. Her lips were an inch from his.

"You might be right about that."

He brushed his lips over hers. A soft, gentle touch that set off fireworks inside her. And she slanted her mouth over his and deepened the kiss.

Her tongue tangled with his and her hands begged to participate. She wanted to touch him . . . feel him . . . break her own rules and strip off *his* shirt.

But then he broke away and sat back in the driver's seat.

"So do you think I won a rose?" he murmured.

She cocked her head. "Do *you* think you earned one?"

"Yes." He lifted his hand and brushed his fingers over her cheek. "And I'm ready for the second date whenever you are, Caroline."

Chapter 5

Josh PRESSED PAUSE on the mental replay of last night's end-of-date kiss. Daydreaming about how much he wanted to slip his hands under Caroline's pretty pink shirt would lead to a reaction that didn't belong in his big brother's kitchen. If Caroline were sitting at the table his big brother had handcrafted . . .

"Planning to make us dinner?" Brody pulled out a chair and sank down.

"I thought Kat was at a conference this week," Josh said as he played Tetris with an assortment of leftovers to reach the beers in the back.

"She is. But Chad is about a minute or two out. He had the day off and gave me a hand on a volunteer search and rescue mission. Another lost hiker. We found her safe and sound." Brody held out his hand for a brew.

"Not for you," Josh said.

Brody raised an eyebrow. "You're stealing my beer? What are you planning to make with it?"

"I'm planning to drink it," Josh said.

"All alone in your apartment?" Chad strode in and claimed a seat across from Brody.

"I'm expecting company." Josh set two bottles on the counter and then returned to the fridge for the lone remaining can. He carried it over to the table. "And I don't have time to go shopping."

"Caroline?" Brody asked as he cracked opened the can. He took a sip and passed it to Chad.

"Yeah."

"You just saw her last night," Chad pointed out.

"Yeah," Josh said. "And we had a good time so I invited her over to watch a movie and share a take-out pizza."

"Moving a little fast, aren't you?" Brody said, reaching for the beer can.

I can count on one hand the number of times I've kissed her this past year, Josh thought.

"She has to work the rest of the week." Josh picked up the bottles. "And I'm done playing games. I wanted to see her so I called and invited her over." He raised his hand holding the beers and pointed first to Brody. "You shouldn't be lecturing me about fast. You were messing around with my doctor on her first night in town." He shifted his attention to Chad. "And you—"

"Lena's different," Chad cut in, his easygoing, playful tone forgotten.

"So is Caroline." Josh lowered his arm. "Stay out of the barn tonight."

"We could always send Katie over to check on the horses," Chad pointed out.

Josh shook his head. "I already told her that I'd let her goats out in the middle of the night if she did that. You'll be out there helping her round them up and making sure they didn't get their heads stuck in the fence again if you encourage her."

"We'll leave you alone," Brody said firmly.

"One more question," Chad added. "What are you watching?"

"Katie lent me that adventure movie about that kick-ass girl with the bow and arrow," he said.

"You can't watch a movie based on a kid's book," Chad said. "Not if you want to get laid tonight."

We could watch porn and the date still wouldn't end in bed, Josh thought. But he wasn't about to explain Caroline's three date rule to his brothers. Or his suspicion that three dates might stretch to four or more.

"I have a better idea." Brody pushed back from the table and stood. "Wait here a sec."

"I'm not watching some cheesy romantic tear-jerker," Josh called after him.

"Afraid you'll cry?" Chad said without cracking a grin.

"Or she will," Josh muttered. He wouldn't run from a crying woman. But their relationship already had a shitload of serious. He didn't need a high-drama movie tossed into the mix. Hell, he would have watched their favorite reality dating show. Too bad it didn't air on Tuesdays.

"Take this," Brody said as he walked into the kitchen

and held out a DVD. "That way you can offer her a choice. Plus, Kat loved this movie. She begged me to watch it with her. I caved and . . ." His big brother raised his hand and rubbed the back of his neck as his gaze dropped to the floor.

What the heck? Is Brody blushing?

"It's a good date flick," his oldest brother added.

"Thanks." Josh took the disc and headed for the door. "But I still think she will prefer the adventure movie."

The screen door leading from the farmhouse kitchen to the great outdoors slammed behind him. But not before Josh heard Chad say, "How come you never gave me porn to share with my girl?"

CAROLINE STARED OUT the window of Dominic's truck. She understood cause and effect. She'd ventured outside her comfort zone and now she felt skittish, as if she should open the passenger door and dive out of the moving vehicle.

But that would be stupid and probably lead to injuries. Then Lily would drag her to the hospital instead of taking her to Josh Summers's place.

"It's nice of you to drive me all the way over here," Caroline said.

"Josh promised cookies, brownies, and a berry pie for the kindergarten bake sale," Lily said. "I can take a couple of hours out of my Tuesday night to give a friend a ride if it means I won't have to slave over an oven this weekend. Plus, I'm happy for you. Getting back out there. Dating again."

"Two dates in two days might be too much," Caroline said.

"After a year of sharing pie, I think you're ready. But I'm only a phone call away if you change your mind. And I'll be back in three hours to drive you home if you don't."

"You don't have to stick around," Caroline protested.

"I'm meeting an old friend for dinner in Independence Falls. It's no trouble. Plus, I want to hear the details of your date."

"We're going to share a pizza and watch a movie," Caroline said. "There won't be much to tell."

Lily turned off the country road and headed for the two-story farmhouse standing beside a bright red barn.

"They repainted," Lily mused. "The house, the barn, it looks good."

But Caroline's heart was beating too fast to take in the details. She waited for the truck to halt beside the lone door on the long side of the barn. Three trucks lined the parking. Four now that Lily had added Dominic's to the lineup.

"They're here," she murmured. "His brothers. Maybe his sister—"

"I doubt Josh invited them to tag along on your movie date," Lily said. "Go have fun. You deserve a night out—or in—with Josh. Plus, I bet he baked you a pie."

Five minutes later, Caroline surveyed the cramped studio apartment over the Summers' family barn. A queen-sized mattress resting on a metal frame filled most of the space. Two doors lined the far wall both open just enough to glimpse a bathroom behind door number one and a closet behind door number two. A flat-screen TV was mounted on the wall. And a table surrounded by a pair of wooden chairs offered the pretense of a dining area in the tiny space.

No pie.

She didn't see so much as a cookie on the counter in the kitchenette. But two DVDs rested on the round wooden table.

"Double feature?" she asked as Josh cracked open a beer and handed it to her.

"My siblings offered their suggestions." He picked up the movies and held out one to her. "I'm guessing you'll like this one."

She glanced down at the familiar image. "Who picked it?"

"My sister." He set the second DVD down beside the mini-fridge and withdrew a second beer. "The girl, she's the hero in the movie, she fights back and kicks some major ass with her bow and arrow." He opened the bottle, raised it to his lips, and took a sip. Lowering it, he added, "She's fierce, tough, and hot. Just like you."

She set the DVD on the table. "I fought because it was my job."

"True, but when you were attacked by one of the good guys, you fought—"

"No, I didn't." She shook her head. "I couldn't. He was my commanding officer. I couldn't fight him."

"But you called him out. You pressed charges."

She picked up the beer bottle and ran her finger over the opening. "Noah called the hotline. The one set up to report situations like mine. He found the number and placed the call. I didn't . . . I didn't even try."

"Caroline," he murmured.

The way he said her name, the pity in his voice—it was as if her past had sent a hand grenade into her second date. And if she didn't remove it fast their evening would blow to pieces.

But she refused to pretend to be some sort of hero. Last night he'd looked at her as if he liked her just the way she was. He deserved to know the truth.

"Protocol dictated that I report the . . ." She couldn't say the word. She stole a glance at the movie cover. She didn't even know the story, but she knew she wasn't the badass with the bow and arrow. And if that was why he'd spent the past year baking for her, if that was why he'd asked her out, he needed to know the truth.

"Protocol demanded that I report the incidents to my commanding officer," she continued. "And really there was no one else. We were on a remote base in the middle of a desert. Cut off from everyone. My family. My friends. Everyone around us would take his side. Except Noah. And he . . . he found a way to report it. He researched the hotline. And he did everything he could to keep our CO away from me. Noah followed me like a shadow whenever he could. It didn't stop . . . everything."

Oh hell, I'm making a mess of our second date, she thought.

"Really," she added softly as she raised her beer to her lips. "It was all Noah."

"No," he said firmly as he set his beer on the counter. "It was you. You survived. You're still surviving."

"I'm running," she said flatly.

He crossed the kitchen/dining area in two strides. "Not right now." His hand cupped her jaw, his touch featherlight and seemingly at odds with his firm tone. "Right now, you're on a movie date."

She let out a rough laugh. "If we start every date like this—"

"We're getting to know each other," he said, his thumb stroking her cheek. "Nothing wrong with that. Now I know you and my sister don't share the same taste in movies. So we'll watch Brody's pick . . ."

He stepped back and she missed the feel of fingers against her skin. His right hand plucked the second DVD from the counter.

"*Magic Mike*," he said.

She laughed as her lips formed a smile that would have felt impossible moments earlier. "Your big brother gave you a movie about male strippers?"

"Yeah." Josh turned the case over and read the back. "Sorry. I didn't look at it too closely. He said Kat liked it. After they watched it . . ." He glanced up at her. "He didn't offer details, but he blushed. And that's rare for Brody. But we can watch whatever is on TV. Maybe there is a reality show? You can look while I heat the pizza I picked up in town. Half cheese, half pepperoni."

"Oh no." She plucked the case from his hand. "We're watching the male strippers."

He shook his head as he turned to the small oven with a pizza box resting on top. "See, I was thinking you would go for the adventure movie. Maybe curl up in my arms and pretend to be scared. We'd both know the truth, but—"

"I'll still curl up in your arms." She removed the DVD and knelt down to insert it into the player. Mike had already worked his magic, banishing the serious from the conversation. "And maybe later I'll talk you into a striptease?"

THANK YOU, CHANNING Tatum, Josh thought as the final credits rolled.

Thirty minutes into the movie, Caroline had set her plate of half-eaten pizza on the floor and sat back against the pillows lining the wall with her shoulder touching his. Then her hand had brushed his thigh as the men on screen thrust their hips in time with the music. And when the show started and he took off his shirt? Caroline had rested her head against his shoulder. He'd wrapped his arm around her and held her close, the side of her body pressed against his.

Who needs bow and arrows when you have male strippers?

"I liked it," he said. "Good message."

Caroline laughed and the fingers resting on his thigh pressed into his jeans. "What message?"

"Following your dreams and all that." He allowed the hand draped over her shoulder to explore. His fingers dipped beneath her neckline of her black scoop neck T-shirt and drew a small circle. "You know, I think Mike will have a really successful furniture business."

"I don't know about that," she said. "If his business takes off, why did they film a sequel?"

"You're kidding," he said, glancing down at her.

She looked up at him and her expression didn't give anything away. She appeared downright somber with her wide green eyes staring into his. And she didn't pull away and tense beneath his touch.

"*Magic Mike XXL*," she said. "I haven't seen it—"

"But now you're dying to know what happens next?"

"I saw a few commercials and watched a preview online," she said. "I have a pretty good idea."

"I guess I know what we're watching on our next movie night," he said.

"You know," she said, pulling away and shifting to sit facing him on the bed with her legs crossed, "I'm not sure I can wait until our next date for more male strippers. Why don't you show me what you've got?"

Her sensual, playful tone, so different from her guarded responses in Big Buck's back room—or the broken note he'd heard earlier when she'd tried to explain how Noah had done what she couldn't when faced with an impossible situation in a damn war zone—left only one response.

Yes, Caroline, I'll take off my clothes for you.

But there was one problem with that knee-jerk reply.

"Caroline, I can't dance," he said. "Not like the guys in the movie."

"Sorry," she said softly. And yeah, he could hear the teasing edge slipping away. "I got caught up in the . . ."

"Heat?" He pushed off the bed and reached for the edge of his T-shirt. He'd pulled the fabric up a few inches before he remembered to move his hips. He rocked them from side to side. He was pretty damn sure he looked like a fool. But then her jaw fell open and her tongue ran over her bottom lip.

"What are you doing?" she demanded. She sounded as if one more hip thrust would send her voice spiraling into sultry territory.

"I'm giving it a shot." He pulled his shirt over his head and tossed it aside. "Stepping out of my comfort zone."

She nodded and her gaze had narrowed in on his stomach. "I've been doing that a lot lately," she murmured.

"Oh yeah?" His hands moved to his silver belt buckle. But instead of freeing his belt, he focused on the hip thrusts, up and back as if he were pushing into her . . .

She'd have to be blind to miss the outline of his dick begging for freedom from his jeans. And judging by the way she leaned forward, shifting her weight to her hands on the bed . . .

Not blind.

She rose up on her knees. "Come here," she said.

He abandoned the erratic movements and stepped up to the edge of the bed.

"Have you ever danced like that for anyone else?" she asked as she placed her palms on his chest.

"No," he growled.

"Good." She leaned closed and pressed her lips to his.

I'm yours, he thought as he released his belt buckle and reached for her. *Your stripper, your date. . .*

His fingers worked their way through her long, loose, wavy hair. He held tight to her as his tongue tangled with hers. He tried like hell to focus on kissing her. But her hands wandered, distracting him as her fingers reached for his belt and dipped beneath his jeans—

Beep! Beep!

The car horn cut through the quiet night. Below them, one of the horses kicked the barn's wall in response. And yeah, he felt like kicking something too.

"I have to go. That's probably Lily," Caroline murmured, pulling away from the kiss. But her fingers continued to toy with his belt buckle. "But I can't wait to see you dance your way out of your pants."

"That's going to be one helluva third date."

Chapter 6

"Josh Summers. Just the man I wanted to see."

Shifting the pastry box to his left hand, Josh raised his right and waved to Noah. "Hate to disappoint you, but I stopped by on this fine Saturday morning to share home-made cinnamon rolls with Caroline."

"She's not in yet," Dominic announced as he pushed through the door that led to the staff only area in back. "She's running five, maybe ten minutes late. Josie's giving her a ride over, but she had to stop and change the baby first."

"Have a seat," Noah ordered in his best don't-mess-with-the-former-Marine voice. He nodded to the line of empty barstools.

Big Buck's didn't open for another fifteen minutes and Josh knew the room filled fast on weekends thanks to the nearby university crowd. He'd never gone the college route, but he supposed that if he had he'd have preferred

to study while sipping a pint of Oregon's finest microbrew.

Knowing he'd have to face the firing squad eventu-
ally, Josh set the box on the counter and claimed a stool.
He eyed Dominic as the soldier-turned-bartender joined
Noah behind the bar. Josh had planned to kick off the
weekend with a sugarcoated kiss in the bar's back room.
Instead, he was getting a lesson in Interrogation 101 from
a former army ranger—Dominic—and Noah.

"You can each have one roll," Josh said as he flipped
open the box. "But the rest are for Caroline."

Noah reached into the box first. "How was your date
Monday?"

"And your movie night on Tuesday?" Dominic added.

"Good." Josh smiled at the large blond bartender who
managed to make the simple act of eating a cinnamon
roll look menacing. But Josh was a long way from breaking under their fierce stares. Though he had to admit
Dominic's dark hair and trimmed beard gave him a leg
up in the threatening department. Add in the fact that
both men played high school football and led their team
to the state championship and you had one hell of an interrogation team.

But Josh had known these guys since they played in
the peewee leagues even though they'd never been close.
They'd lived in different school districts and their home-
towns were about an hour apart. It cut into the intimida-
tion factor.

"Where did you go on Monday?" Dominic asked as he
examined the box's contents.

"Caroline didn't tell you?" Josh added a hint of feigned shock to his tone.

Noah shook his head. "Caroline told Josie that she should have worn her combat boots. But that's it. So where did you take her? The local pizza place in Independence Falls?"

"For a first date?" Josh raised an eyebrow. "No, I went with someplace more romantic. And private."

He watched Noah bite down hard on the soft, fluffy pastry. And yeah, it was difficult not to laugh. But Josh managed as he plucked a roll from the box. He'd tasted one at home, but he had a feeling this conversation might drag on a while. The smell was too damn tempting to resist a second. If he had a third with Caroline, well hell, he'd hike it off later. Or maybe dance it off while he stripped down for Caroline . . .

Dominic rested his forearms on the polished wooden bar. "Just how private are we talking?"

"Are we really doing this?" Josh asked.

"Answer the damn question," Noah said.

"I'm just saying, if we're suddenly 'BBFs' and all"—Josh paused and took a bite of his roll—"we might want to break out the nail polish before I fill you in on the down-and-dirty details from my dates."

"What down-and-dirty details?" Dominic growled.

Josh grinned. "Well, things got pretty wild in the hot tub."

"Fuck," Noah muttered.

"Not that wild," Josh said, trying to add a note of o-woe-is-me to his voice. "But I have high hopes for next time. And don't worry, I'll tell you *everything* at our post-date sleepover."

And now you laugh, Josh thought. But the army ranger and the Marine had packed away their sense of humor for the day.

"Look, Josh, I've known your family a long time," Noah said. "And you seem like a good guy. But I swear—"

"I see," Josh cut in with a nod. "This isn't a heart-to-heart talk."

"If you hurt Caroline, if you push her to do something she isn't ready for, we're going to have problems," Noah continued.

"I know," Josh said. "And while I'm willing to bet I can hold my own seeing as I grew up with two big brothers, we're on the same page. I won't push her. But I also won't treat her as if she's broken. She went through hell and she doesn't need you, me, or your sidekick"—he nodded to Dominic—"acting like it defines her. She deserves to be wined and dined away from curious stares so I took her to my favorite vineyard for a sunset picnic on Monday. And we watched a movie my brother recommended on Tuesday. If you want to know more than that, you'll have to ask her yourself."

The door to the back room swung open and Caroline marched in. She spotted the three men gathered around the bakery box and ground to a halt five paces from the bar.

Josh sat back on his stool and took another bite of his roll while he admired the view. She'd traded the borrowed boots for her preferred footwear. The I'll-kick-your-ass combat boots matched with her don't-mess-with-me expression, but not so much with her fitted jeans and long-sleeve Big Buck shirt. This top hugged her curves compared to the oversized work shirts she usually wore.

"Ask me what?" Caroline demanded.

"The down-and-dirty details from our date," Josh said.

Her gaze honed in on the pseudo-interrogators behind the bar. Sure, they'd been looking out for her. And Josh appreciated that fact. The more people on Team Caroline the better. But he also hoped she gave them a little hell for crossing the line.

"I missed the locker room chat?" she asked.

"It wasn't like that," Noah said.

"He's right. Nothing like that, sweetheart," Josh drawled. "These boys are more of the bonbons and brunch type."

"And here I thought they'd *promised* to stay out of my business," she said with a sharp look at Noah.

"Don't worry, I'm making sure they remain true to their word," Josh said.

She walked over to his stool and rested one hand on his thigh. He glanced down at her fingers resting on his jeans. As a rule, she didn't invite physical contact in public. He'd learned to respect that barrier. Hell, he'd kept his hands to himself during their picnic. He'd been granted a good-night kiss before she climbed out of his truck, but even then he hadn't dared touch her. And he'd waited for her to make the first move after the movie. He wasn't in this for the score, and he sure as shit didn't want her hopping into bed with him to banish bad memories. He needed her to desire *him*.

But none of that changed the fact that he welcomed her hand on his leg right now. And he didn't give a damn about the former state champion athletes standing on the other side of the bar.

"So you didn't tell them about the hot tub?" she asked.

"Nope." He shook his head and fought back a grin. "They don't need to know how you earned your rose, my sweet. Some things should remain private, you know?"

Including any and all references to my Magical post-movie performance, he thought.

"So true," she murmured as she withdrew her hand. "But I think it's fair to tell your buddies here how much you enjoyed the theme of the movie, right?" She glanced over the bar at Dominic and Noah.

Josh nodded and tried to match her solemn expression.

"Josh really took it to heart," she added. "He was rooting for the hero in the end."

This woman's wry wit might push me over the edge.

He liked her. He'd been damn clear about that. But this could snowball fast with emotions piling up before their third date.

Without warning, she placed one foot on the metal base of his stool and climbed onto his lap. His arms went around her slim waist and held tight. Across the bar, Josh caught Noah's wide-eyed stare and knew he was just as surprised by her move.

"Relax, Noah," she said. "I learned the three date rule

in high school." And she reached into the box and pulled out one of the rolls he'd made just for her.

"You might need to clarify that one for Noah. He didn't exactly play by the rules when he started courting Josie," Josh said before Noah could jump back into the conversation.

"No, he didn't," Caroline said.

Noah shook his head and muttered something about opening up for paying customers as he walked away. His sidekick took one more roll from the box and turned to the half-empty tray of clean pint glassware. With his back to them, Dominic stacked the glasses.

"I should get to work," Caroline murmured.

"Finish your breakfast first," Josh said. Even though prolonged contact with her perfect backside would probably leave him with a hard-on that would linger and leave him aching.

"Mmm," she murmured as she took another bite. She leaned back against him and that's when it hit him. She'd playfully sparred with Noah and shocked them all when she'd climbed onto his lap, but she wasn't playing defense. She felt relaxed in his arms.

"Caroline?" he said in a low voice.

She glanced at him over her shoulder, her lips lined with white icing from the roll, and he thought what the hell? Second chances were for going after the girl who made him feel like he'd found his future, right? And if he was open and honest with her, if he took his time, they could make this work. Sure, her problems were big. But he refused to believe this—them, together—was destined for failure.

With his arms still wrapped around her waist, he hugged her close. His lips grazed her ear. "I don't give a damn if Noah loosens up. But I enjoy seeing you like this. Relaxed. Carefree. Whenever you're ready for that third date, just say the word."

She licked the icing off her lips. And yeah, there was no way she'd missed the large, imposing fact that she'd turned him on. His dick was close to bursting out of his jeans and begging for entry into hers.

"I have a dinner break before my evening shift," she said. "Five o'clock."

"I'll be here."

CAROLINE PUSHED THROUGH the swinging door and tried to school her expression.

Don't think about Josh.

If she started skipping through the bar with a rack full of clean glasses while remembering how he felt pressed up against while she sat on his lap—large and eager—she would draw attention.

Her chin dipped to her chest and her shoulders hunched forward as if trying to make herself disappear. She stole a sideways glance at the nearly empty barroom. No one was looking at her. The small groups of college and grad students hadn't stopped midsentence to wonder who the woman with the dishes was.

AWOL. Outlaw. Fugitive.

Pushing past her comfort zone didn't change the fact that those labels hovered over her. They rose up like a solid brick barrier to a long-term relationship with Josh. Part of her ached to reach the third date and beyond, but after that . . .

Josh wanted the massive timber-frame house on the hill, the loving marriage, and probably the two point five kids to complete the American dream. She didn't hold that against him. She believed in that vision of Americana bliss. She'd fought to keep that hope alive. Or at least that was why she'd joined up. She'd wanted to be one of The Few. The Proud. The Brave . . .

But it didn't feel very brave to fight her commanding officer for her sense of dignity, for her right to dictate who touched her and how. And she wasn't proud of the fact that she'd lost that battle.

The familiar tension rose up and pulled at her shoulders, threatening her nerves. She'd spent most of the week thinking about her dates with Josh. The way he'd teased her at the end of that first night when they'd pulled up to Noah's childhood home, now her sanctuary . . .

Do you think you won a rose?

He tossed the question out there. She'd turned the tables and tossed it right back at him. He hadn't laughed at the idea that other men would fight for the chance to date her. He'd simply said yes.

But her life wasn't a reality TV show. They could have dozens of heart-to-heart conversations and when they finally moved passed kissing, when they finished the striptease they'd started in his apartment, she might leave the ghost of her bravery behind and run.

She stumbled and nearly dropped the rack of glasses.

"Too many cinnamon rolls?" Dominic asked.

"Josh baked and I missed it?" Lily turned to her boyfriend. "And you didn't save one for me?"

Dominic shook his head as he lifted the slab of wood that kept the patrons on their side of the bar. "Can't have you admiring another man's buns even if they're made of cinnamon and sugar."

Dominic and Noah appeared at her side both reaching for the rack of clean dishes. But she held tight, glancing from one man to the other. "It takes two of you to handle a dozen customers?" she challenged. "Or are you waiting around to give Josh a hard time again?"

"Ryan's stopping by with Helena," Dominic said as he plucked the rack from her arms and turned back to the bar.

Caroline took a step back. She wasn't eager for more getting-to-know-you chitchat with an officer who lived and breathed the world she'd left behind.

"Helena was his best friend since they were in kindergarten," Noah explained. "She wasn't able to make the wedding. Something to do with her husband's prior commitments, but she's in town for a quick visit and wanted to stop by."

"I'm so glad Ryan talked her into a trip. I haven't seen her in years," Lily mused. "I know she wanted to get far, far away from her mom's farm, but it's like she moved to California and never looked back."

"You don't need to worry about her, Caroline," Noah added. "She was always a little wild and never played by the rules. The cops in this town are probably still looking for Helena in connection to half a dozen pranks."

"Helena's a lot of fun," Dominic added as he pulled glass after glass from the rack and arranged them in a neat line. "We used to go four-wheeling out on her mother's farm." He glanced over his shoulder. "You would have had fun if you'd joined us, Lil."

Lily gave a fake shudder. "Getting covered in mud was never my idea of a good time. Unlike Helena, I didn't want to find clumps of hay in my hair the next day."

"I would have helped you wash your hair, Lil," Dominic drawled.

Lily laughed. And Caroline tried to use the moment to slip away. She would rather have a conversation with the now empty industrial dishwasher than an air force officer.

"Looks like we're late to the party," a familiar male voice called.

Lily caught hold of Caroline's arm. She glanced down at Lily's bright pink nails. "You don't have to go," Lily whispered. "Stay and meet Helena. You'll like her. And you already know Ryan."

Caroline nodded and took a step back as if she could disappear into the shadows. But the area near the bar was well lit, unlike some of the corners behind the subwoofer stacks near the DJ stage. Still, the new arrivals weren't looking at her. They were focused on their friends—or at least the man in air force dress blues was too busy shaking Noah's hand to notice her. The woman—Helena—she kept her gaze fixed on her shoes.

No one rushed forward to greet her. Noah, Dominic, and Lily—they all stared at her. And Caroline could understand their hesitation. They were probably scared they'd wrinkle her because the mud-loving, four-wheeling farm girl looked like she'd walked off the pages of a fashion magazine. From her Prada stilettos to her fitted white Capri-length jeans to her tailored pale-pink blouse, this woman looked like she would scream and run if she saw a cow.

As for mud or hay in her hair? Caroline couldn't picture the newcomer with a single strand of her blond bob out of place. She was sleek, slim, and wearing enough makeup to keep her face looking picture perfect from morning till night, and probably beyond.

For the first time since she'd arrived in Forever, Oregon, Caroline felt like she might fit in here. Sure, it was only by comparison to the long lost Helena. Still—

Ryan stepped closer to the Prada Princess and went to put his arm around her. The perfect, put together woman flinched as if he might hit her. It was a small movement. Maybe the others hadn't noticed, Caroline thought, because a split second later, Helena allowed her best friend from childhood to drape his arm across her shoulder.

Ryan gave her a tepid squeeze and then withdrew his hand. One look at the officer's face and Caroline suspected he'd seen his friend react as if he might hurt her. The tall man in the dress uniform appeared equal parts hurt and mystified.

But Caroline knew. Looking at Helena . . . it was like staring into a mirror and seeing her own reflection from a year ago. Not the clothes or the hair, but the way Helena held herself apart as if she craved isolation—as if she wanted to make herself somehow less. The clothes were a shell, but they didn't offer this woman assurance. If Helena had been sure of herself at some point, her confidence had been stripped away.

Caroline didn't know this woman's story. She doubted Helena's childhood friends knew the hows and whys behind her transformation. But she recognized that island of complete loneliness. She'd lived there and she knew without asking that Helena hadn't brought herself to this place.

Chapter 7

CAROLINE SLIPPED INTO the back room while the circle of high school friends struggled to make small talk with their old friend. The questions echoed in the nearly empty barroom and drifted through the swinging door.

Did she like California?

Yes.

Had she made new friends?

Some.

Helena was the queen of stiff, one-word answers. When asked if she worked, she told them she'd tried acting, but then she'd met Ashford. And she'd given up the starving artist life when she married him. Helena punctuated the explanation with a laugh that sounded like it had been tried and tested at country club cocktail parties—or maybe in her old acting classes.

But the visit continued, moving in stops and starts. Helena asked a few questions about the bar before slipping back into her stunted responses when Lily pressed for more details about the amazing Ashford. He worked in the catchall field of 'business' and liked golf.

Laughter spilled in from the front and Caroline wondered if she'd imagined the other woman's loneliness. Maybe talking to Josh about how she'd felt trying to navigate through a world where the man who was hurting her maintained his position of power had led her to project her feelings. She'd never met this woman before. And while she could tell Helena had changed after she'd moved away, that didn't mean—

The door leading to the bar's public space swung open and Caroline instinctively moved closer to the dishwasher. But Helena clearly hadn't rushed out of the bar's front room to see her. The Prada Princess held her cell phone pressed to her ear.

"I'm sorry," she pleaded, her voice trembling. "I didn't know you were taking an earlier flight—"

From halfway across the room, Caroline heard a male voice shouting what sounded an awful lot like *you left without telling me. I didn't give you permission.*

Why would Helena sneak away to visit her hometown? And why would she need permission?

The rest of the words were lost, but she clearly heard "you bitch" and "come home now."

"Yes," Helena said. "I will." Then she closed her eyes and lowered the phone. Tears streamed down her face.

It was none of her business, but Caroline stepped forward, her steel-toed boots pressing into the squishy rubber mat that covered the floor beside the dishwasher.

Helena opened her eyes and turned to her. "I'm sorry," she said quickly. "I didn't realize—"

"You don't need to apologize to me," Caroline said. "Are you all right?"

"Fine." She wiped at her eyes, smearing her mascara over and around her eyes. "I just need to freshen up. Is there a bathroom back here?"

"If you need help—" Caroline began again.

Helena forced a smile. "I'm sorry you heard our little fight."

"That was an attack."

Helena's mascara-rimmed eyes widened. "No," she said firmly. "I forgot to tell him that I'd planned a quick trip up here. I just forgot . . ."

It was a lie. She'd heard the way the man on the phone barked the word 'permission.' He controlled her. Whether he hurt her physically or just used his words, it all amounted to the same thing—abuse.

"You don't have to go back," Caroline said.

"Yes, I do," she said.

And maybe Helena was right. Maybe she did need to return to Ashford. Maybe leaving him wouldn't solve anything. After all, running away had delivered Caroline to world of new problems.

"I can't leave," Helena continued, but this time her voice broke over the words. "He'd come after me. He'd stop sending money to my mom. And . . . he doesn't hurt me."

"Helena?" Ryan's voice called from the front. "There's a limo waiting outside for you."

"Be right there," Helena called back, her tone suddenly light and upbeat.

She should have stuck with acting, Caroline thought.

But rewriting the past was impossible. And in some cases, so was moving on.

Helena's gaze darted around the room. "The bathroom?"

"Over there." Caroline pointed to a door on the far side on the room near the desk. "Take your time," she added. "I'll tell them you'll be out soon."

"Thank you," Helena whispered, the falsely positive note gone from her voice.

Caroline shook her head. "You don't need to thank me. I don't think I'm helping you."

But Helena had already locked herself in the staff bathroom.

"WHAT THE HELL happened to her?" Noah demanded when Ryan marched through the employee entrance to the bar.

"A designer clothes explosion," Lily murmured.

"I haven't seen Helena since before I left for basic training," Noah continued. "But I swear, if I saw her walking down the street, I wouldn't have recognized her."

Caroline closed the dishwasher and set it to run. Then she turned and headed for the group surrounding the air force officer. Noah, Dominic, and Lily had left Josie in charge of the now open bar to have a 'serious conversation' with Ryan after he returned from walking Helena out to meet her limo driver.

"She sure as shit isn't the same Helena we knew in high school," Dominic said. "I know people change. Hell, we all have. But not like that."

"She died her hair blond," Lily added. "Her beautiful, long brown hair. And I couldn't even see a single freckle beneath all that makeup."

Because her husband told her to, Caroline thought.

The group of old friends stood near the door leading to the employee parking area. A wall lined with beer cases and kegs, some filled and others empty, occupied the space beside the group. And the desk, covered in stacks of paper, lined the far wall by the door leading to the employee bathroom Helena had used to pull herself back together.

But no one was looking at the mess—or even sparing her a glance. They were all focused on Ryan, waiting for his answer.

Ryan shook his head. "I don't know. But I'm planning to go to Palo fucking Alto and figure out what the hell is going on. I should have gone years ago when she stopped visiting her mom. Or letting anyone go down there to see her. I called her mother after she rushed out of here and jumped in that damn limo. Helena's mom hasn't been down to see her in four years. It's never a 'good time' for her husband."

"Shit," Noah said, shaking his head.

"And I got the sense her mom doesn't want to make waves because Helena sends money every month," Ryan added bitterly. "They never had much, but to bury your head in the sand to your daughter's problems in exchange for a paycheck?"

"That's a little harsh," Lily said. "You don't know the full story. Helena might be perfectly happy—"

"He's hurting her," Ryan growled. "I don't know if he's hitting her. But he's doing something."

"Sure that's not jealousy talking?" Lily asked gently.

"Ryan's never had a thing for expensive clothes," Dominic said.

Lily narrowed her blue eyes at her boyfriend. "I meant jealous of Helena's husband, what's his name."

"Ashford," Ryan spat out.

"At your going away party," Lily continued, turning now to Ryan. "The night before you all left—"

"Nothing happened," Ryan said. "We started messing around. Last night in town and all, but it felt too weird. Like kissing my sister. So I ended it and got the hell out of there, pulling my damn shirt back on as fast as I could. And afterward . . . I always figured that's why she kept her distance. Maybe it felt too weird. Maybe she needed space. And then she got married."

"You think her husband hits her?" Dominic said. He didn't raise his voice. But there was an undercurrent of steel in the former army ranger's tone.

"He's doing something," Ryan growled. "She cut her hair for him. Dyed it for him. I asked her about it when I picked her up at her mom's place. She said, 'Ash likes it.' She didn't laugh once on the drive over."

"You can't walk away from the air force on a hunch," Dominic said.

"He's right," Caroline cut in. She couldn't keep quiet, standing by and listening while they explained Helena's problems away. It was too easy. She knew from experience.

Sure you didn't send mixed signals? Are you certain you didn't flirt with him?

Almost everyone Caroline had told about Dustin tried to minimize or shift the blame. Some held the military culture responsible. And some placed the fault on her shoulders.

Of course that was different. She'd come forward. Helena had stood in here and told her she was 'fine.' She'd said her husband wasn't hurting her.

But Helena still felt she couldn't leave. And that wasn't right. Everyone should have the right to walk away.

Caroline drew a deep breath and told Helena's friends about the phone call and their conversation afterward.

"That's it," Ryan snapped. "I'm going down there and I'm bringing her back here. If he tries to come after her—"

"How much more leave do you have?" Dominic demanded.

Caroline rested her hands on the stainless steel table that separated the dishwasher from the rest of the storage room/office. She suspected she knew his answer. The thought of hearing those words sent a chill down her spine.

"I'm not going back," Ryan said firmly.

"You can't go AWOL," Noah said without looking at her.

"What do you plan to do when you get there?" Dominic demanded. "Have a chat with her husband? You'll need to hang out for a while to get a sense of what is going on. And if you're wrong, you'll be in a helluva lot of trouble."

"He's right," Noah added. "You can't walk away from the air force to follow up on an old friend. I'll go."

"And leave your wife and child?" Ryan shot back.

Caroline walked around the edge of the stainless steel table and headed for the bickering group. "I'll go," she announced, standing behind Lily.

Four heads turned toward her.

"What?" Ryan's movie star brow furrowed. "You don't even know her. Just because you overheard her talking to her husband—"

"I do know her." Caroline kept her tone strong and even.

"What the hell? Are you from Palo Alto?" Ryan cocked his head.

She shook her head. "I know how she feels. Alone. Afraid. I've been there. Most days, I still am. I can help her."

Maybe.

But she suspected she had a better shot than Ryan. He might love her like a sister, but he still loved her. And bonus, Caroline had already tossed away her military career.

"No," Noah snapped. "You can't go, Caroline."

"Looks like I missed the party." Josh's happy-go-lucky voice sliced through the tension as he pushed open the door leading to the staff parking area. "Change your mind about letting her take a dinner break, boss?"

"Your girlfriend just volunteered to visit California," Lily said.

Josh turned to her and raised an eyebrow. "We're going on a road trip?"

"No." She looked straight into his beautiful green eyes. "Just me."

"Forgetting that you don't have a car or a license?" Josh said. "I happen to have both. And a pile of vacation days ready and waiting to take my girl on a trip."

"I'll manage on my own. I don't need to drag you into this."

Or the little side mission she'd been plotting since Ryan first announced his intentions to follow Helena to California.

It had been over a year since she'd run away fearing Dustin was hot on her trail, ready to turn her in—or worse. And listening to Helena, she'd realized that running came with its own issues.

She needed to see for herself that her former CO no longer posed a threat. On her way down to Palo Alto, she planned to swing by Dustin's hometown. But no one needed to know that part of her plan.

"So you're dumping me?" Josh asked. "Before the third date?"

"Josh—"

"I don't pretend, Caroline." He pushed through the group and headed for her. Lily stepped aside to make room for him.

She could have backed away. Ran. But no, she was done rushing off at the first hint of fear. And Josh didn't frighten her. Although if she stepped back and thought about his public insistence that they were honest to God dating she might say . . .

Yes, join me.

He stopped within arm's reach and raised his hand. His finger brushed her right cheek. "And I have a rule about letting my girlfriend walk or, hell, hitchhike across state lines."

"You and your damn rules," she muttered.

He smiled and lowered his hand. "I'll take that as a yes. When do we leave?"

"Tomorrow. First thing."

He nodded. "I'll pick you up at seven. And I'll bring the coffee and doughnuts. Seeing as this will be our third official date and all."

"Before you go," Ryan jumped in. "We need to talk."

"I'm listening," she said, keeping her gaze fixed on Josh while Ryan demanded to know her plan.

Josh had changed into a long-sleeve, button-down shirt for their one-hour dinner date. He'd dressed up for her. He liked her. But if they had any hope of moving beyond 'like,' she needed to face her past. She would knock down her fears one by one on this trip. And then maybe they would have a chance at something more. She would still face the threat of arrest. But a fugitive's happy-ever-after was better than nothing.

She glanced at the man who'd traded his go-to flannel for a dress shirt. She'd heard him talk about his siblings. His brothers and sister had their ups and downs on their way to happy-ever-after. But now they were living the dream—Josh's dream. There was even a rumor that his oldest brother, Brody, planned to adopt a child soon. And she knew for a fact his sister was expecting her first child in five or so months.

Would her constricted version of love be enough for him?

Chapter 8

WHAT AM I *doing driving to California on a pseudo-rescue mission?*

Josh mulled the situation as he raised his travel coffee mug to his lips. His brothers had asked that question ten different ways when he informed them of his plans to take a road trip.

Sure it's a vacation when your girlfriend's carrying a loaded gun?

His oldest brother, Brody, had added that one to the pile. And no, Josh wasn't sure of a damn thing other than the fact he couldn't let Caroline run off to help a woman she'd met for five minutes. If that truly was her number one reason for heading back to the part of the country she'd run from once.

Plus, he wanted a third date.

The door to Noah's old farmhouse swung open and Josh focused on the porch. His girlfriend appeared with her backpack slung over one shoulder. She'd tied her long dark hair back in a bun. And she'd selected cargo pants, her combat boots, and a plain black T-shirt for their adventure.

"For the record," he said as she pulled open the door to his truck, "I liked your fitted jeans better. Although I suppose those pants offer more room for your gun."

"They do." She settled into the passenger seat, her pack nestled between her feet.

He held out the box of doughnut holes. "In that case, I'll let you have first pick. Take all the chocolate ones if you want."

"I prefer the ones with the jelly filling." She reached into the box and took three white powdered doughnuts.

"Really?" He set the box down and handed her a cup of coffee. His fingers brushed hers and he thought *that's why I'm here*. He wanted to touch her, talk to her, and learn about her doughnut preferences.

He put the truck in gear and backed out of the long gravel drive. "I hate the jelly-filled ones," he added.

"And I know you love chocolate," she said in the same sensual tone she'd used the other night when she told him to strip.

He slowed to a stop at the top of the drive and glanced at her. "Tell me you'll marry me."

"So that we can spend the rest of our life sharing boxes of doughnut holes?"

Yes, he thought. *And moonlit walks through vineyards. And dirty movies. . .*

She popped a jelly-filled one in her mouth and shook her head.

"Too presumptuous for the third date?" His grip tightened on the wheel as he turned onto the road and headed for the highway.

"Let's see if we survive the road trip first." Out of the corner of his eye, he saw her look at him. "Did you map out the route?"

"We could do it in one day," he said. "Nine to ten straight hours in the car. But I thought it might be nice to pause and stretch our legs once or twice."

She nodded as she stretched out her legs in the passenger seat and turned her gaze to the window. "I need to make a stop about an hour, maybe two, south of the state line. I'll direct you once we get closer."

Tell me more about how you like your doughnuts. But he knew he had to ask about the little side trip she'd dropped into the conversation.

"To see your sister?" And yeah, he wished he could see her expression, but he had to keep his eyes on the road. "Don't tell me we're skipping straight to the meet-the-family dates."

"Not this trip." She let out a forced laugh. "She's still upset that my former CO showed up at her doorstep and started tossing out threats while her kids were in the house."

"Your sister blamed you for that?" he asked with a healthy dose of what the fuck in his tone.

"She was scared. But we weren't exactly close before. And since I ran, she's started talking to my parents," she said.

"Your parents," he repeated. Any trace of humor had exited the conversation as they sped down the highway.

He'd spent hours with her in the back room at Big Buck's. He knew that she'd grown up moving from one base to another. Her father had been a Marine. And he'd always assumed they'd passed away. She'd talked about her sister. Her niece and nephew. But never her mom and dad. He'd never pushed because shit, he didn't talk about his mom much. She hadn't been in the picture for a long time and he left it at that.

"They're back in Maryland," she said. "Or that's what my sister said the last time we talked. She wanted to know where I was. She said my parents had been asking. But if they knew . . ." She sat up straight, her hands folded in her lap and her chin held high. "They'd turn me in."

Josh punched the gas and fought the urge to swerve off the road and park on the shoulder. She had a group of people—a sort of family—at Big Buck's who'd worked to keep her secret. But her own parents would see her locked in a jail cell.

"Why?" he said, his voice low and hard.

"They believed my CO," she said. "Or at least my dad bought into the 'good soldier' defense and in the end it was my word against Dustin's. He admitted we'd had an affair. With Noah's testimony, he couldn't skirt that issue. But Dustin claimed it was consensual."

She listed the facts as if the trial had happened to someone else. Her tone remained calm. But one glance away from the road, and he saw the tension in her posture. She sat up straight, her shoulder blades drawn down her back. And her legs were no longer outstretched in front of her. Her feet rested on either side of her backpack.

"His defense countered that the traumatic environment altered my perception. We were on a remote base, close to what many considered the front lines of the battle. Everyone was tense all the time." She shrugged. "My dad believed the decorated soldier, not me. And my mom followed my father's lead."

"They didn't fight for you." It was a statement, not a question.

"No. I guess in their eyes I wasn't a good enough soldier."

He reached over and took her hand. "I think it takes a helluva lot more courage to do what you did, to speak up against the person everyone sees as the 'good guy' than to stand by the lines drawn in the sand between good and bad."

"Thank you," she murmured.

He squeezed her hand, but kept his eyes on the road. "And I stand by my assessment from the other night. You're more badass than any other woman I've ever met. And I find that so damn hot."

She laughed. And another quick peek told him that he'd won a smile.

They drove in silence for a few minutes. But the questions lingered. And he couldn't push them away. If they weren't stopping to see her sister, where did she want to go?

There was only one other person he could think of from her life before she'd run away to Forever. Her rapist. And shit, that put one helluva dark spin on their third date.

"So this stop in Northern Cali. Are you planning something that might get you arrested?" he asked.

She pulled her hand free from his. "No."

But once again there was a boatload of serious in her tone. His brothers might have been right about this little trip redefining 'vacation.' And he hated to let his brothers win. Ever.

"Look, I don't have a lot of experience with road trips. In fact, this is my first time outside of Oregon."

"You're kidding. No family car outings as a kid?"

"My mom left when I was little. My father did his best for us. But he was a sane man. He never tried to load the four of us into a car and take us across state lines. We visited the coast once or twice for clamming, but that's it. He worked a lot to make ends meet. There wasn't much left over after paying the bills and trying to keep us all fed for fancy vacations. You've seen a lot more of the world than I have."

She let out a brittle laugh. "I know there are beautiful places in the Middle East, in Iraq and Afghanistan, but I don't think the US military posts are on the top sightseeing stops."

"Probably not," he acknowledged. "Where would you go if you could go anywhere?"

"I can't. If I use my passport—"

He pushed away the rising need to erase 'can't' from her vocabulary. He'd pull the truck over right now if he could tear down the hard limits she put on her life. He knew the complexities of her situation couldn't be tossed out the window and abandoned on the side of the Oregon highway. "But if you *could* go somewhere?"

"What is the point in dreaming about something you can't have?" she said softly.

"Situations change. One day—"

"There's no 'one day' in my future. We both know that, Josh. If I try to board a plane bound for Hawaii, I'll be arrested."

"Why Hawaii?" he asked.

He glanced over and caught sight of her full lips pressed tight together. "You're annoying. You know that, right?"

"My sister reminds me all the time. And you agreed to spend the next few days in a car with me."

"Few days? It's a nine- to ten-hour drive."

"I thought we'd break it up, maybe work in a modified version of your dream beach vacation. That's why you want to see Hawaii, right? The beautiful beaches? Or were you interested in the volcanoes? Oregon has those too."

"The beaches," she murmured, turning her attention to some distant point out the window. "And I want to see the ocean. But—".

"If we have time to stop in Northern Cali before we head south to rescue a woman who might not need our help—"

"She does," Caroline said firmly.

"I believe you. But if we have time to visit your number one enemy—"

"I didn't say—".

"Wild guess," he said dryly. "If we have time for that asshole, we can take a detour to the scenic route and spend the night by the beach."

"Sleep on the sand under the stars?" she murmured.

"If that's what you want. I was thinking more along the lines of a hotel with a view of the water. Maybe a balcony."

"Josh, I've spent the past year washing dishes. Noah's been generous, paying me more than he should, but—"

"My date. My treat. Two rooms with a view of the ocean," he said firmly. "Plus, I'm hoping you'll be so relaxed that you'll forget all about stopping to visit the past."

"I can't," she said simply.

Yeah, he'd been afraid she'd say that.

"Caroline," he said. "There's nothing but trouble waiting for you if you try to see him. What are you hoping to get out of this side trip? An apology? He owes you a helluva lot more than that. And from what you've told me, what Noah's told me, I wouldn't put it past the bastard to call the police if you show up on his goddamn doorstep."

"I'm not going to talk to him—"

"Good," he said firmly.

"But . . ."

Josh sighed. Yeah, he'd known there was a 'but' at the end of that statement.

"I need to know once and for all if he's after me," she added.

"All right," he said grudgingly. "But I'm going with you."

She nodded. "Of course."

He reached for the radio and tuned to the first station he found that played something other than country. "Now sit back and enjoy the ride. Imagine how the sand will feel between your toes."

Chapter 9

CAROLINE SURVEYED THE exit routes while Josh secured their rooms. But mentally mapping the hotel's exterior from the truck proved challenging. Three large brown rectangular buildings surrounded the parking area and the rooms lining the three stories all faced out. The ones on the far side had a spectacular view of the water while the others looked out on rows and rows of parked vehicles. She could hear the ocean beyond the structures, but she'd have to get out of the truck if she wanted to see the waves.

Glancing around the empty parking lot, she opened the passenger side door and slipped out. She headed for a cement path between two buildings filled with guest rooms. Carefully maintained grass covered the ground behind the hotel leading to a row of thick hedges.

"I have good news and bad news."

Josh spoke from behind her. He wasn't close. Not yet.

And she'd spent enough time with Josh to know that he possessed a healthy respect for her personal space.

"What's the bad news?" she demanded, her mind running through worst-case scenarios. The hotel staff had demanded her government issued identification . . . The oceanfront resort was out of rooms so they'd have to sleep in the bed of the pickup . . .

"Just a minute, Ms. Doom and Gloom, I'm starting on a high note," he said. "See that structure down there? Just visible beyond the hedges, directly on the sand?"

She nodded. The small triangular cottage looked as if one big wave might wash it away into the sea.

"That's ours for the night," he said. "Secluded and right on the beach. You can't see it from here, but there is a porch on the front. Plus, it comes with a kitchenette."

She nodded slowly, trying to process the fact that he'd rented her a private cottage so close to the water that high tide probably touched the porch steps. It wasn't a villa at one of those fancy Hawaiian resorts, but it was a lot to take in for a third date.

"What's the bad news?" she asked, remembering his earlier warning.

He turned to face her. "There's a conference at the main lodge and they're booked. The cottage was the only opening. There's a queen bed and a sleeping loft. I'll take the loft, but it's an open floorplan apart from the bathroom. If the loft is too close for comfort, I can grab a sleeping bag from the truck and camp on the porch."

You can sleep in the loft, she thought. *I'll be fine.*

She knew that was the logical response. He'd paid for

the cottage. But she hadn't slept that close to a man in a long time. No walls. No safe barriers. Not that she needed them from Josh. Part of her wanted to propose they share the bed.

And part of her wanted to lock him outside for the night.

"That should work," she said slowly. "But I might change my mind and claim the porch. I've never slept this close to the ocean before."

He held out a key. "Why don't you head down and check it out. I'll grab our bags."

Her fingers touched his and she grabbed his hand. "Thank you, Josh. For bringing me here. But I need to make one thing clear."

He nodded.

"I'm picking the location for our next date. It probably won't be a beachfront cottage because I'm on a budget, but—"

"I'm up for anything." His lips curved into a full-blown smile. "Go enjoy the view."

CAROLINE WALKED OUT of the bathroom with her long black hair wrapped in a towel and Josh knew he'd be spending the night on the porch. His call. Not hers. And it didn't have a damn thing to do with the towel—or the fitted jeans that hugged the curve of her hips. Or the loose, thin sweater material that played peek-a-boo with her breasts. It was a black *sweater*, not thin strips of silk for Christ sake, cut in the shape of an oversized men's dress shirt minus the buttons and collar. One look shouldn't inspire a roar of lust.

Ah hell, I had a hard-on for her when she wore over-sized T-shirts and baggy cargo pants.

He glanced out the cottage window. If Caroline traded her loose-fitting outfits for lingerie, he'd have a second, maybe two, to make the call before lust overrode his brain and body. Run for the sand dunes or let her seduce him?

But he didn't have to make the choice tonight. Her sexy sweater wasn't exactly a secret of old Victoria's. And he'd tossed the idea of moving past second base out the window during their long drive. Not long after he'd turned on the radio, she'd drifted off to sleep. He'd focused on the road, putting more and more miles behind them. But he couldn't stop replaying their earlier conversation.

I need to know once and for all if he's after me.

He remembered the trigger-happy woman who'd nearly shot a raccoon not long after she'd started working at Big Buck's. But over time, she'd let the paranoia slip away. Or maybe she'd learned to hide it. Either way, she wanted closure.

He felt a lot of things for this woman. Admiration and lust topped the list. But he also knew that he couldn't go to bed with her to help her slam the door on the past. He wasn't afraid she'd freeze or he'd touch her in a way that triggered a memory of her rape. Although, shit, that was something they'd need to address too. But if that happened, they'd stop and deal with it. He wasn't backing away from her because he feared the stop-and-starts or scary moments that led to more talks instead of climaxes.

But if they reached the let's-get-naked date, he planned to have a long discussion with her before they lost their clothes. And he suspected that would be hard on both of them. He'd parted ways with 'serious' long before his accident. His eldest brother, Brody, had always been the somber one. Chad had picked up the playboy label and run with it—until he met Lena.

And that left Josh with humor.

But a talk about how to avoid triggering memories of the way she'd been raped didn't call for laughter and it couldn't be avoided. He supposed he could breathe a sigh of relief since that chat wouldn't happen tonight. Not because he wasn't feeling as if his jeans had shrunk a size or two since he'd watched her emerge fully dressed in an oversized sweater.

He needed her to want him in the same crazy-for-you-even-if-you're-wearing-a-baggy-old-sweater way he wanted her.

His erection threatened to object—

"The shower is all yours." She released the towel and let the long, wet strands of hair tumble over her shoulders.

He relinquished his place on the tiny love seat shoved into the one-room cottage's kitchenette in an attempt to create a 'living space' between the bed and the front door.

"But I used all the cold water," she added as she pulled a hairbrush from her backpack.

"That's all right. I'm fine with . . ." He paused in the

doorway to the bathroom and turned to her. "How did you manage to use all the cold? As the youngest, I know for a fact that the hot goes first—"

"I was teasing you." She offered a rare wry smile. "Something"—she let her gaze drift south and settle below his belt—"told me you might need a cold shower."

He let out a laugh, but didn't turn away from the spark of sexual awareness. He was already headed for a cold shower. "Before our *third* date? Don't worry, Caroline, I haven't lost count."

"Me neither," she said softly.

Maybe I should rethink my plans to sleep on the porch, he thought. But he shook his head and headed for the cold shower he desperately needed now.

"There's a bottle of Oregon pinot noir on the windowsill by the mini-fridge," he called back to her. "I also picked up some dinner for us. The coast's famous clam chowder."

"I'll warm it up." She nodded to the bathroom. "I'll meet you on the porch when you're done with your shower."

He walked into the cramped space but couldn't resist adding: "If this was our fourth date, I'd invite you to join me. But naked time in the shower on the third? That's against the rules."

"You're right," she shot back. "No shower sex before the fourth date. But hot tubs are excluded from that rule."

He let out a laugh. "Wrote these rules in your spare time?"

"No," she said. And he heard the door to the mini-fridge slam shut. "We have the gods of reality TV to thank for their insights into the ritual of dating."

"You watch too much television," he said as he closed the door and rested his hands on the vanity's edge.

But he could have sworn he heard her add, "But I don't live under a rock. Not anymore."

Chapter 10

THE WAVES RUSHED over the grey-white sand, teasing the three steps leading up to the porch. From her perch on one of the four all-weather metal chairs beside the table, Caroline studied the water as it slipped back. She imagined the tides washing away the lingering effects of the past few years. The beach beneath the water had been disturbed, shifted by the waves' movement, but the sand remained a solid surface.

She cocked her head and turned her gaze to the sun slipping below the horizon. If she was comparing her life to the ocean's movements she'd probably had too much wine. One high tide wouldn't strip her past and leave her with a fresh new start.

But Josh offered living, breathing proof that trouble could slip away. He'd regained his footing and then some after his accident. He smiled and appeared so comfortable in his own skin. And tonight, he'd laughed freely while they debated just how much 'reality' went into their favorite shows over steaming bowls of chowder.

"Josh." She tore her gaze away from the orange-gold sky and looked at her date. "When did you start watching reality shows?"

"Would you believe me if I told you it was a life-long passion?"

"No."

He grinned. "The nurses at the rehab center liked them. The ones on the night shift always wanted to watch dating shows. I enjoyed their company. Hell, some days it felt like the only thing that kept me sane."

"How did you know?"

"One of them gave me a journal during my first week and told me to write everything down. I still have it. Minus the pages Chad took back."

She raised an eyebrow.

"He stopped by to pour his heart out when he and Lena hit a hiccup in their relationship. I honestly can't tell you more than that because he tore out the pages."

"Did it help?" she asked. "Keeping the journal?"

"Yeah. It's weird waking up in what feels like a strange new place every day, not knowing the people around you, only to learn that you've been there for weeks."

"I can't imagine," she murmured.

"I don't think anyone ever really understands what another person is going through. The nurses tried. But most nights, even after their stupid memory game therapies, I didn't want to sleep. I felt lost in my own life with no way out. So I started watching whatever the nurses wanted to see. Of course, I forgot about it the next day. But months later, when my memory came back and I'd moved into the apartment over the barn, I started tuning in again."

"Out of habit?" she asked.

"Nah, I wanted to know why I'd written about roses and hot tubs in my journal." He set down his wine and looked her straight in the eyes. "Now I need you to promise you won't tell my older siblings. They probably think I'm watching porn up there and we should keep it that way."

"Promise," she said solemnly. "But I get to pick the drive-thru for tomorrow's lunch. Or I'll call up your sister and tell her—"

"Deal," he said quickly. He held her gaze as he reclaimed his glass and took a long sip. "Now how about you? Did you sit around at the base and watch TV?"

"No." She shook her head and looked away, staring out at the sand. "My sister is a reality show junkie. She had it on all day. From pregnant teenagers to people willing to eat bugs for money, she liked it all."

"I've never seen the appeal of eating bugs on national television," he murmured.

"Me neither," she said with a laugh. But it sounded forced, even to her ears.

Why can't I have a normal conversation with this man? she wondered. But given her situation, maybe this was normal—the best she could hope for anyway.

"But your sister liked those shows," he prompted.

"Yeah," she said, mentally tossing normal out into the

surf as she added: "And when I was staying with her, I couldn't leave the house. I knew it was only a matter of time before the police came to her door and demanded to know if she'd seen me. So I stayed inside and watched with her. I waited for the inevitable . . ."

But it doesn't feel so inevitable right now.

She closed her eyes. Witnessing the sunset, following the water's ebb and flow, and sitting beside a man that infused her life with wanting, she'd felt as if possibility hung in the air—as if her new version of normal was within arm's reach. She'd set out to face her past. To see for herself if Dustin was interested in hunting her down. If he wanted to seek revenge for a career he'd lost most than a year ago.

Damn it, I wish I could take out my past with a single shot. One well-aimed bullet and the reasons I ran, even the fact that I decided to go AWOL instead of serving with those bastards again—I could blow it all away.

"Look at me, Caroline," he said softly. "Please."

She opened her eyes. Her date looked downright serious. And yes, that was on her. Josh laughed openly and freely. He seemed happy just about all the time. Except for when she started unpacking the baggage from her past.

"Even at my lowest point," he said, "when depression clouded my life and I thought my short-term memory was gone, I didn't stop hoping. And that I remember clear as day. You haven't hit a dead end. Trust me on this. I know you. Not who you were before or all the details about your family. But I know that if someone as strong and brave as you gives up, the rest of us don't stand a chance."

"I don't know what to wish for anymore." She rolled her shoulders up toward her ears and then down. "Every time I think about the future, this tension seeps in. I feel it lodge between my shoulder blades like a physical reminder that I'm tethered to my past actions."

Josh rubbed his hands together. "Now, this is going to sound like a come-on designed to advance tonight into the tried and true third date parameters. You'll just have to take me at my word that my motives are sixty percent pure."

"Only sixty?" she said with a laugh.

"Yeah. Now, here it goes." He cleared his throat. "Sweetheart, I can ease that tension right here, right now with a little back massage," he said in a deep voice that sounded like a cross between used car salesman and Magic Mike.

She laughed again. And he waggled his red-gold brows.

"What about the other forty?" she asked.

"Sinful." He shook his head as if ashamed to admit part of him leaned toward ulterior motives. "But I think I can keep those impulses in line long enough to relieve that ache in your back, honey."

"All right." She plucked a cushion off one of the empty chairs as she stood. As she walked around the table, he pushed back and created a space for her at his feet. She dropped the pillow to the wooden boards and sat with her back to him and her gaze fixed on the horizon.

His hands rested on her shoulders. The wide neckline of her knit sweater offered access to her bare skin and he took advantage. His fingers slipped beneath the fabric and his thumbs ran down alongside her spine. Then, without a word of warning, he began to massage her tight and tired shoulders.

The pure pleasure of welcoming another's touch rippled through her. And thank you, angels in heaven, he didn't break the moment by asking if she was all right, or if he made her uncomfortable. Josh trusted her to speak up and tell him if she needed him to stop. But still, it probably wouldn't hurt to add a little encouragement.

"Please don't stop," she murmured.

"Wasn't planning on it," he said.

He used his knuckles to target the pockets of pure tightness underneath her shoulder blades and she moaned.

"I'd forgotten how good this feels." She didn't give a damn if her voice bordered on low and throaty. The pleasure had clearly migrated south, drawing her attention to the parts of her body that no longer wished to be ignored.

"Keep reminding me," he said. "Or my imagination might talk my hands into wandering."

"Where?" she teased.

His fingers slipped over her shoulder and ran down the front of her shirt. He stopped below her collarbone. Tracing gentle circles over her skin, his touch gliding back and forth under her bra strap, he said, "I'd start here and work my way lower."

She arched her back, offering access and encouragement. "Then?"

"My hands would slip under your bra and cup your breasts."

"Hmm," she moaned. But his actions didn't mimic his words. He continued to massage her pectoral muscles.

"And then I'd face this inner struggle," he continued. "Do I lift your breasts and press them together or tease your nipples first? If I run the pad of my thumb over your nipples, I could gauge how you like to be touched and learn if your breasts are sensitive. And I should probably start there. Because if I draw your tits together first, well hell, I'd be tempted to dip my tongue between them and lick my way to your nipples."

His words painted an X-rated picture in her mind of a scene that belonged inside the cottage—bedroom, love seat, or sleeping loft, it didn't matter as long as they slipped behind a closed door. Just in case someone walked down the beach. She had a list of her own unexplored fantasies, but they didn't involving attracting outside attention.

"I can tell you've lost sleep over this debate," she said.

"Caroline, you don't want to know how much I've fantasized about your cleavage." He added a serving of sincerity to his tone as his finger dipped lower, grazing the top edge of her breasts.

"Tell me."

"But then you'll think I'm only concerned with your breasts. And that's just not true."

"Right now, I'm just interested in how my breasts play into your wildest daydreams." She ground out the words as she arched further. She cocked her head to the right and rested it on his knee. "Please, Josh."

He let out a soft chuckle. "Are you sure about that? Because once I finish licking a path between your tits, I'd

kiss my way over that taut little belly down to your panties. And this time there's no debate. I'd touch you first,
testing to see if you're wet, before running my tongue
over you until you came."

She drew a sharp inhale as her body responded to
his words. See if she was wet? If he kept talking, she'd
be tempted to slip her own hand into her underwear. It
wouldn't take much before her cries left anyone out for a
sunset beach walk wondering if the cottage offered a different kind of view.

"All this time and I had no idea you had such a dirty
mouth," she said, her voice different, but not unfamiliar—at least not to her ears. But it had been a long time
since she'd been this turned on.

"That's that forty percent of pure sin." His hands
stilled on her shoulders. "Sorry—"

"I like it."

And he wasn't the only one with a sixty/forty split.
Although right now, the balance was tipped in favor of
her naughty side.

"But I think it's your turn." She lifted her head off his
knee and pulled away from the hands that had begun
kneading her shoulders again. She pushed off the porch
floor and turned to face him. "Sit down, Josh."

"You're going to give me a massage?" he asked, raising
one beautiful eyebrow.

"Don't sound so surprised." She waited for him to
shift from the chair to the cushion on the floorboards.
"You spend all day wielding a chainsaw and hauling big
heavy logs out of the forest."

He laughed as he settled on the pillow and stretched his long, jean-clad legs in front of him. "Here I've been baking for you, trying to win you over with sugar and whipped cream, and I could have taken you out to a job site and revved up my chainsaw."

"Well, if you want to talk about fantasies . . ."

She let the words linger on the crisp night air. One glance at the ocean suggested the sun would disappear below the horizon any minute. Darkness would follow along with a reason to move inside.

She glanced down and tried to focus on the tan skin dipping below the neckline of his T-shirt. Under or over his shirt she wondered. Or . . .

"Would you mind slipping off your shirt?" she asked. "I don't want to stretch out the neckline."

He laughed again as he reached for the fabric at the base of his neck and drew the shirt over his head. "You know if I tried that line, it would sound dirty."

She placed her hands on his naked shoulders. "I'm just getting started."

A long time had passed since she'd looked at Josh and thought *imposing*. That first night, in the clearing, his broad shoulders and tall, muscular form had appeared threatening. But now the formidable expanse of pure muscle beneath her hands impressed without frightening her.

Probably because he's sitting at my feet. And I've seen him perform a striptease.

Her fingers dug into the taut, hard plane of pure male perfection. The man beneath her touch moaned.

"Too hard?" she asked.

"No," he growled. "Go deeper."

Her hands ached as she kneaded his back, winning another low groan. By the time she worked her thumbs lower, pressing against the outline of his spine, he was practically purring. And for the first time in years, she felt a ripple of power threaded with desire.

She trailed her fingertips over his skin and she felt him shiver. Placing her palms on his shoulders, she ran her hands down his biceps. The muscles flexed beneath her touch.

"I've daydreamed about your arms." She spoke in a low voice, but kept her tone matter-of-fact. She wasn't trying to seduce him beyond this moment. She simply wanted to explore the body she'd admired for months. "Even before your little *Magic Mike* dance."

"Tell me," he murmured.

"But how will you ever manage to share a brownie with me in Big Buck's back room if you know I've imagined what it would feel like to run my hand over your chest?" Her fingers followed her words, gliding up over his shoulders and down his chest. Red-gold chest hair greeted her hands.

"I like chocolate," he said. "And I like sharing it with you."

"Sometimes," she murmured as she dared to take his massage a step further and trace circles around his nipples, "I wondered what would happen if you ditched your flannel button-down after everyone else left. On those nights when you stayed to make sure I got home safe after a long Saturday night shift."

He let out a low growl of approval.

"Josh, I've wanted to explore your body for a long time. And I didn't envision stopping when I reached your belt buckle."

He cocked his head and glanced over his left shoulder, green eyes dancing with amusement. "All this time we were sharing brownies and pies, talking about how many pint glasses the bar went through on a busy night, and you were fantasizing about my dick?"

"Wondering," she corrected. "Imagining how much you had to offer."

He gaped at her. Whether from surprise at her blatant words, or shock that someone with her past would mentally debate his intimate dimensions . . . Well, she hoped it was the former. Because he'd never treated her as a victim. Yes, he'd abided by her boundaries. But she'd chalked that up to good manners and a healthy respect for women.

"I didn't think—" he began. "I didn't realize—"

"That I still think about sex?"

"That you were mentally undressing me while you worked," he said with a smile.

She returned her hands to his shoulders and began to massage him again. It was surprise, pure and simple. She'd added the layers. "You didn't realize that your fantasies lined up with mine?"

"If I'd known, I'd have withheld the pie until you told me everything."

"I have a feeling I could have talked you into sharing a slice or two," she said.

He leaned back into her touch. "Tell me what happens after you strip off my pants . . ."

"First, I take a long, hard look—"

The first few notes of 'Sweet Caroline' cut in. Josh scrambled to his feet and dug his cell out of his jeans front pocket.

"Shit," he cursed.

The song played another bar. *That's for me*, she thought. But why now? Why here? Plus, she didn't have a phone. Unless it always rang like that . . .

"When did you change your ringtone?" she asked.

"This one's set for Big Buck's." He swiped his finger across the screen and held the phone to his ear. "Hello?"

She wrapped her arms around her waist and tried not to stare at his crotch. His jeans didn't hide the fact that he had a lot to offer.

Next time, she thought. *After I pay Dustin a visit.*

But he was ready now . . . and he'd programmed his phone for her.

"Hey, Noah. Yeah, she's right here. I'll put you on speaker."

"Where are you guys?" Noah's voice boomed through the phone. "Are you close to Palo Alto?"

"Not exactly," she said with a glance at the receding waves still visible under the rising half-moon.

"We took a detour to the coast," Josh added. "I thought Caroline needed a little time with the ocean. Some fresh air and all before we head south."

"That sounds great," Noah said. "But shit, Ryan's going crazy. He's called twice since he got back to base.

And look, he believes Helena needs a full-blown rescue mission. "

"She does," Caroline said. "And she's going to get it. We're on our way."

"Great," Noah said with a sigh. "I'll pass the message on to our air force friend."

"Has he called her?" she asked. "If he has reason to believe her situation has escalated, Ryan might want to call the local police. We can go and talk to her, offer a way out, but there is no guarantee she'll take it unless she's desperate."

"If she was dying to escape, she could have stayed in Forever when she had the chance," Noah pointed out.

"It's not always that cut-and-dried," she said simply.

"I know," Noah said. "Trust me, I know."

The line went silent. She suspected Noah—the man who'd tried his best to save her from an officer who should have been fighting beside them—was taking a brief trip down memory lane.

"Enjoy the beach, Caroline," Noah added finally. "And thanks for turning this into a real vacation for her, Josh."

"Yeah, I just tagged along to prove that I rock at dating," Josh said easily. "We found this resort by the sea. A cozy, beachfront cottage. Nice clear night—"

"I've heard enough," Noah said. "Keep me updated on your mission."

The call ended and Josh pocketed the phone. Then he bent down and reclaimed his shirt. He must be freezing by now. Fall nights in Oregon called for sweaters, not bare chests.

"Sounds like we should get an early start," she said as she stood and picked up her chowder bowl.

"You know we might get down there only to have Helena slam the door in our faces." Josh scooped up his dishes and followed her through the cottage's front door. "Noah's right. If she wanted help she could have stayed with her mom."

"She could have," Caroline admitted as she set the bowl in the kitchenette's tiny sink and stepped aside to make room for Josh to do the same. "But she spent about twenty-four hours in her hometown. That's not a lot of time to shake the feeling that there is no escape."

"Still, she had a way out," he said. "She could have moved back home."

"Maybe Helena felt that she couldn't. We won't know until we talk to her. I do know that it's one thing to be hurt by a stranger. But someone you know and trust? Like the man she swore to love until death do them part?"

"It's different." He crossed his arms in front of his chest. The posture highlighted his biceps, but she didn't feel like exploring his muscles now. Not when his expression was set to 'dead serious.'

"I felt like there was no way out. No escape." She wanted to look away, but forced herself to meet his gaze.

"Yet you're going back to see Dustin," he said. "Funny how you left out that little detour when we were talking to Noah."

"He doesn't need to know," she said. "And we'll be at Helena's tomorrow night."

"But you think Helena feels she can't get out," he said.

"Someone needs to build the path for her and then show her the way."

"I'm glad you escaped," he said with a sigh. "But are you sure we're the right duo for the job, this 'rescue mission'?"

She nodded slowly and waited for his smile to return. It was as if he'd left his grin, his laugh, and his charm on the porch. "But if you're having second thoughts—"

"I'm going with you," he said firmly.

"Don't want to miss out on another date?"

His muscles contracted, accentuating his powerful arms. But still no smile.

"Caroline—"

"Would it help if I made us a pair of superhero costumes?"

And finally, *finally*, his lips curved up as his gaze headed south. "Would you wear one of those spandex outfits? The ones cut like a strapless bikini? And those knee-high boots?"

She crossed the small kitchenette/living room space and tapped her index finger to his forearm. Fighting the temptation to continue her earlier exploration of all his hard-earned muscles, she rose up on her toes. Her lips hovered an inch from his.

"Be careful what you wish for," she murmured. "Or you might find yourself wearing a pair of tights with your cape."

"I'm willing to take the risk." He lowered his mouth and captured hers. Her body hummed, eager to join in and make this a full-body kiss. His lips moved over hers, but he stopped short of reaching for her. Slowly, he pulled away and stepped back. And she lowered her arms to her side.

"Good night, Supergirl," he said. "I'll be on the porch dreaming about your legs in those crime-fighting boots."

Chapter 11

No escape.

Despite all her talk about superheroes and sexy costumes, those words repeated over and over like the refrain to a song Josh couldn't get out of his head. Hell, he swore he saw the letters spelled out in the sky as he stared up at the stars.

He had a hard time imagining the bold, beautiful Caroline trapped by anything. Wearing a sparkly leotard and fighting crime? Hell yeah. But never defeated.

Maybe I put too much faith in her strength.

He glanced at the door leading to the cottage's warm and snug interior. He didn't mind the cold night air or the wooden floorboards beneath his sleeping bag. He'd wanted to give her space. And he'd needed some himself.

What if his brothers had been right? The idea practically gave him hives. But still, he had to wonder if this little road trip was destined to implode. He knew what he wanted for his future. And driving around the coast with his girlfriend was a far cry from settled down. Add in the fact that she wanted to spy on her rapist and this trip seemed destined for failure.

The past is best left alone. Better to move on.

He'd learned that lesson over and over. When his mother left without looking back, when an accident stole weeks of his life, literally wiping them from his memory. Yeah, he knew better than to look back.

Plus, he'd witnessed his brothers' struggles on their way to love. Chad had been up front with him after Josh's breakup with Megan.

I let my abandonment issues hold me back when I fell in love with Lena.

And Josh had laughed until his sides hurt. He'd wished he'd recorded his brother, the former town playboy, talking about his feelings. But when he told Chad to repeat himself word for word so that he could capture his statement, his older brother had threatened to kick his ass.

Just don't fall into that trap.

That was Chad's final bit of advice. And it had taken Josh a while to receive the message, but he'd finally made the call. Time to get serious and settle down. Only he didn't share his brother's 'issues.' His mother was part of the past. He didn't linger on the memory.

But he knew it wasn't that easy for Caroline to let go. Maybe tomorrow's trip down memory lane would help. Maybe it would sever the connection. Or maybe her 'issues' were too big.

No escape.

Josh closed his eyes. He knew what he wanted. A fourth date. Caroline in his bed—or hell, the front seat of his truck. But he didn't want to be her escape. He wanted to be her home—her second chance at a future that wasn't marked by fear and failure.

And I wouldn't turn down another massage. . .

His body responded to the memory. But he didn't reach beneath the sleeping bag to ease the ache. That was one feeling he wanted to linger, ready and waiting to play out their mutual fantasy.

"PLANNING TO CHANGE into your costume on the road?" Josh held out a steaming cup of coffee. He'd woken early and fought his way through the hotel's convention crowd to secure two cups of joe and a box of pastries for the road.

"I didn't want to run the risk you would be distracted while driving." Caroline accepted the cup and climbed into the passenger side of the truck. Settling her backpack at her feet, she opened the pastry box and peered in. Then she selected the jelly doughnut.

"Too late for that," he said as he buckled into the driver's side. "My imagination is already running wild with images of those kick-ass boots."

With her free hand, she picked his cell up from the center console. "I'll pull up the directions while you day-dream about Wonder Woman."

"She always was my favorite," he admitted. "Chad

preferred Catwoman, but I liked to stick with the good guys—and girls. Plus, with Wonder Woman, what you see is what you get. Catwoman always had a trick up her sleeve."

"You know that Wonder Woman was really an Amazon princess right? And she had a third identity she used for her day job," she murmured. He stole a quick glance at her and saw her attention still focused on his phone.

"A lot of people behave one way at work and another at home," he said. "I'm not too crazy about the cat villain's whip."

"Oh really?" And he recognized the playful note in her voice. "You don't have a secret desire for a spanking?" she added.

Out of the corner of his eye, he saw her set the phone on the dash with a hint of a smile on her lips. "No. But Wonder Woman's golden lasso might be fun."

"I'll keep that in mind," she murmured. "Take a right up ahead and then merge onto Highway 101."

"Are you going to fill me in on the plan or should I just change into my special spandex outfit when we get there and follow your lead?" he asked.

"Which one did you bring?" she asked.

"Superman. But I tossed in my Batman outfit at the last minute just in case you have a thing for super wealthy men out to save the world." He waggled his eyebrows but kept his gaze fixed on the road.

"I'm not into heroes." The outside of her hand brushed his thigh as she reached for her coffee cup. She lingered for a second before picking up her cup. "You can keep your jeans on."

"You can save yourself?"

"I do my best," she said firmly.

He shook his head. And to think he'd questioned her strength last night. "All right, but I'm still coming with you today. So how about filling me in?"

She inhaled, sucking the air through her teeth. "I want to drive by Dustin's house," she said finally. "He lives outside Eureka, not far off this highway. Just stay on this road."

"Are you still keeping tabs on him?" He stole a quick glance in her direction. Through the passenger side window, he could still see the ocean crashing against the coastline.

"Remember that private investigator Noah hired last year? Back when he thought Dustin was after us?"

Josh nodded. He'd spent a number of long nights hiking through the woods near Noah's house and searching for the bastard. Hell, he'd been shot at by the man after Josie. And at the time, he'd thought it was Dustin. Though Josh didn't like to spend too much time pondering his second close encounter with a potentially life-ending event.

"The PI sent us Dustin's address after his wife kicked him out. She'd moved off base during the trial. And when he was found guilty of adultery . . ."

He let out a growl that made it pretty damn clear what he thought about the fact that her rapist had been charged with freaking cheating instead of rape.

"His ex-wife wanted to be closer to family I guess. Either way, Dustin moved too. He stayed close enough to see his kids. And lucky me, I was hiding out with my sister. He knew enough about my background to hunt me down."

"And you think he's still there?" Josh asked. "It's been over a year since the PI located him."

"Some days I still think I see him hiding in the trees," she admitted. "But I'm fairly certain that's my fear acting up and playing tricks on me."

"You haven't mentioned this," he said. "Have you told Noah?"

"He has enough on his plate. New baby. New wife. And I think we can both agree my paranoia has caused enough trouble for him."

"Caroline," he said. "I doubt seeing Dustin, finding out where he is and what he's doing, will erase those fears."

"We'll find out."

He nodded.

"I have a feeling he's around here. I hate the man, but I know for a fact he loved his kids. Although his wife might still have a restraining order against him."

"Please tell me you're not planning to approach him and talk to him."

"I don't know," she said. "I don't think so. I mainly just want confirmation that he's moved on and living his own life."

"So this is more of a recon mission?" he asked dryly. "We'll sit in the truck with a box of doughnuts and stare through our binoculars?"

"Disappointed?"

Yes, I'd been looking forward to throwing a few punches at the man who hurt you. I wanted to kick his ass for not understanding that one simple fucking word—'no.' And I'd hoped he'd give me a reason to break his damn nose for sending you into hiding.

"Nah, I didn't want to spend our fourth date in jail. I was hoping to finish my *Magic Mike* dance. It might get awkward if we're sharing a holding cell with the local drunks. Plus, I agreed to let you pick the spot."

"I had something in mind." She withdrew another powdered pastry from the box. "Of course now I need to find a golden lasso. And that might prove challenging."

"Did I forget to mention my number one rule?" He shifted in his seat as his lower half took a sincere interest in the conversation that had, thank freaking goodness, moved away from Dustin the Asshole. Talking about boots and superhero sex toys turned him on instead of leaving him itching for a fight.

But the chances of making love to Caroline tonight, after she saw once and for all that her past was sitting on his ass in Bumblefuck, California, might be slim. He should probably resign himself to a long drive with a hard-on for company.

"What rule?" she asked.

"No bondage until the sixth date." He added a hint of mock regret to his voice. "And I know you're a stickler for the dating rules."

"I am."

She sounded so damn serious that he took his eyes off

the highway for a second to make sure she was smiling. But her full lips and big green eyes didn't give anything away.

"So I should probably ask if you have any restrictions on black lace on the fourth date," she said. "You see, I ordered this pair of panties online back when I first asked you out."

His grip tightened on the wheel. Make that two of them who'd had enough talk about the effects of her past.

"You're wearing them now?" he demanded.

"Yes."

Blood rushed south. He never let desire rule him. Not with Caroline. But damn it, he felt primed to explode. He wanted to touch her, kiss her, and make her *his* right here on the highway just from thinking about her underwear.

He couldn't. But that didn't stop him from hitting the brake and steering onto the shoulder. He threw the truck in park and turned to her. "Are you playing some sort of game designed—"

"No games." Her fingers reached for the button at the top of her cargo pants. She lowered the zipper an inch and slipped her right hand inside. He followed her movements.

Don't tell me we waited a year and now we're going to lose control and play show-and-tell on the side of the road.

He could refuse to join in. But as soon as she drew a thin strip of black lace into view, he decided to let her make the call.

"Do you like them?" she asked.

And how she managed the question without a hint of

coy come-and-get-me in her voice . . . hell, he didn't know and he didn't care.

"Caroline, I fucking *love* your panties."

And I'm falling in love with you.

He'd known it since Noah and Josie's wedding. What he felt for her was so damn real and right. And yeah, it was part of why he'd followed her on a rescue mission road trip. Why he couldn't risk another look at her underwear until he was damn sure she wanted *him*, not an escape from her fears. Just him—beneath her, inside her, on top of her, behind her . . .

I'm going to lose my mind on the side of the road.

"You sure chose one helluva day to debut those undies," he said, returning his gaze to her face. Those big green eyes, that heart-shaped face—she looked so damn innocent.

This is the wood nymph side. He'd seen a lot of her *G.I. Jane*, ready-to-kick-some-serious-butt side lately. But she wasn't all hard lines and rough edges.

"Sure you don't want to change our plans for the day and drive back to the cottage?" he asked.

"I can't do that." She zipped up her pants. "Just remember all the reasons we don't want to end up in a jail cell, OK?"

"Caroline, for the rest of the day, your panties will be front and center in my mind. And I promise that if I start thinking about throwing a punch or two, I'll take a deep breath, close my eyes, and imagine sinking to my knees and running my hands up your bare thighs to that slip of black lace—"

"Please."

He pressed his lips together. She wasn't begging. No, she'd offered the plea like a command.

"If you plant one more tempting image in my mind, I'll ask you to stop the car," she said. "But I can't stay here. I need to keep going."

"I know." His right hand released the wheel and reached for hers. He touched her fingers before grabbing hold of her hand. "I swear I won't say another dirty word until you're ready."

Chapter 12

CAROLINE FOCUSED ON the changing scenery outside the window. They'd parted ways with the Pacific Ocean not long after they'd crossed over the Oregon-California line. The trees loomed larger and more imposing as they headed closer to Eureka. Picturesque towns continued to dot the windy road, but she'd stopped noting the names.

I don't feel like Wonder Woman anymore.

She'd abandoned turned on hours ago, not long after Josh steered the car back onto the road. And she'd tossed empowered and sexy out the window after California's famous redwoods replaced the Douglas firs. The reality of what she was doing, driving closer and closer to a man who might be waiting to hurt her . . .

Logic—and a detailed private investigator's report—told her that Dustin had never tried to hunt her down after that one threatening visit to her sister's home. She doubted he'd let go of his anger. And she still woke up wishing he were in a jail cell instead of roaming free. But he hadn't contacted her sister or her again.

Still, I'm here. In California. On his turf. . .

If he saw her, he might come after her. But if he did, she'd kick his ass. She would put an end to this. She wasn't powerless. She was no longer under his command. And she didn't answer to him.

Of course a fight could land her in jail. And a run-in with the local law enforcement would lead to a stint in a military prison for her. Not exactly her ideal location for a fourth date.

"We're getting close to the exit," Josh said.

"Ready to stretch your legs?" she asked.

He'd been behind the wheel since they left the cottage this morning. She glanced at the dashboard clock.

Only two hours had slipped by? Anxiety was like a time warp, drawing out each minute, making the seconds feel like ticking time bombs.

"I thought this was just a drive-by," he said as he shifted into the right lane and veered off the scenic highway.

"You can stand beside the car and eat your doughnuts," she murmured as the muscles in her shoulders formed tight knots. The memory of Josh's massage, the feel of his hands working to ease her body's determination to stand guard, her need to be ready to fight or flee . . . that memory flew away.

They drove in silence listening as the strange female voice from Josh's cell phone guided them through California suburbs.

"Arrived at your destination," the phone announced.

"Thanks, Siri," Josh muttered as he pulled into the parking lot beside a two-story apartment building.

"He's in unit 1B. First floor." After reading it over and over, searching for a clue, she'd memorized the investigator's report. She reached for the truck door. "Let's go take a look."

"Hold up a minute." Josh placed his hand on her arm. "I don't think this is a good idea. We can't just walk by the guy's home and peek in his windows."

She leaned forward and withdrew a battered Seattle Seahawks baseball cap from her backpack. "I borrowed it from Noah's dad," she explained as she pulled her ponytail through the back of the hat.

Josh raised an eyebrow. "We need to work on your superhero disguises."

"Most people only see what they're expecting to see," she said. "And I doubt Dustin's been looking over his shoulder, wondering if I'm waiting outside his window. As much as I wanted to, I never threatened his safety. And believe me, there were nights when we were deployed that I wanted sneak into his bunk and hold a knife to his . . ." She stole a glance at Josh. "Well, not his throat."

"Caroline, I've wanted to threaten this asshole with the blade of a knife since I met you. And I'm being completely honest when I say that I've never had an interest in touching another man's junk." He cocked his head. "What stopped you?"

She shrugged. "He was bigger and stronger. He'd overpowered me before and I knew he could do it again.

Also, he'd trained in hand-to-hand combat and he slept in a room filled with men who would have taken his side."

"I would have taken yours," he said, leveling her with a hard, fierce look. "I am on your side. You know that, right?"

She nodded.

"I want to hurt this asshole. But I have a personal interest in keeping you out of jail," he continued. "So I have to ask. Where's your gun, honey?"

"Locked in its case," she said with a regretful sigh. "And tucked in my pack. I thought it would be too tempting."

"Let's keep it there," he said. "Now I'm ready for a walk by if you are."

The steps bled together—getting out of the truck, taking his hand, and walking up the sidewalk—and she focused on the rush of adrenaline. She refused to acknowledge the fear. It had been the same when she'd driven a truck down a road potentially lined with IEDs in the Middle East. Focus on the rush of energy. Hone in on the mission.

They walked up the cement path leading to the front of the pale yellow building. Steps from the strangely pleasant looking structure, the path divided, leading to two separate ground level units. Stairs ran up both sides providing access to the second story.

A brown cardboard box stood in front of the door on the right. Caroline stopped and stared at it.

Just a box. Not a threat.

The door to the unit on the left swung open and she turned her attention to their destination—unit 1B. But the young blonde in the doorway wasn't her target.

"Hi there," the blonde called as she shifted a toddler clutching a stuffed penguin to her other hip. "If you're looking for Angela, she moved out last week. Her mom's ill so she picked up and went home to San Diego. But I'm forwarding her mail if you want me to tell her that you stopped by."

"Hello," Josh said, firing up his charm. He grinned at the woman in the doorway before turning his smile to the shy child in her arms. "I'm Brody."

Oh really? she thought.

"We're not looking for Angela. My girl and I were just passing through and wanted to look up an old friend," he continued.

Or spy on him...

"Do you know Dustin?" he asked. "He lived in 1B—your unit—a while back."

The blonde shook her head and shifted the child a second time. "Sorry, he must have moved on. I've been here six months and I know everyone."

Josh wrapped his arm around Caroline and pulled her close. "I told you we should have called first, sweet pea," he said in mock chastisement.

She nodded and turned to the nosy mother who hadn't offered her name. "Sorry to bother you. My silly idea to drop in on him. Back to the truck, *honey pie.*"

With Josh's arm still wrapped around her, she spun

on the heel of her combat boot and headed for the truck. "You should stick with logging and baking," she muttered. "Your acting skills need work."

"Yeah, I've never been good at lying," he said as he unlocked the passenger side door and held it open for her. "But at least we confirmed that he's moved on."

She nodded as she climbed into the truck. The door closed and she took one last look at the sunshine-yellow building.

Dustin wasn't there.

A fresh wave of fear hit her and threatened to draw her under. It was a like a current that could hold her down until her lungs begged for air. But she fought back drawing a sharp inhale.

Inhale, my ass. That was a sob.

And if she didn't get herself together, another would follow. Tears would flow. And once they started, she'd lose her last vestige of control. She'd melt into a weeping, wailing mess. She knew the way down that path. She'd followed it before, dissolving into a crying mess in the bathroom stall on a remote military base in Afghanistan while Noah waited outside determined to escort her safely back to her bunk.

She'd been prepared to fight on those nights too, but instead she'd run up against failure. Just like today. Her eyes filled with tears, but she fought to hold them back.

Don't cry!

She looked away from the house and fought to control her breathing. Dustin hadn't been here for six months. But if he wasn't here, where had he gone?

JOSH WAS PRETTY damn sure closure didn't lead to a stoic, teary-eyed Marine sitting still as a freaking statue in his passenger seat. And if he didn't act soon, she would *really* begin to cry. He'd known her for over a year. He'd rushed to Caroline's aid after Josie was attacked in Noah's barn not long after she appeared in Forever. He'd removed a shaken Caroline from the scene when the police showed up. He'd witnessed wild panic in her green eyes but never anguish. And she sure as hell had never shed a tear in front of him before.

"Where to next?" he asked. "Do you have another address for him? Work? Maybe his ex-wife?"

Action. She needed to focus on doing something. Looking forward, taking that next step—it was the only way to fight back when life seemed hell-bent on pressing the 'overwhelmed' switch. Hadn't he learned that the hard way, moving from one damn game to the next hoping he'd be able to reclaim his memory? In the end, he'd recalled only the feelings, the frustration, but never the events or games. Some nights he'd been close to tears too.

Caroline nodded and reached for her pack. Withdrawing a manila folder with worn edges, she flipped through the pages. "His ex-wife lives nearby. That's the only other address in here."

"Work?"

She shook her head and drew her lower lip between her teeth. For a second, he thought she'd start crying in earnest.

"No," she said finally. "When Noah hired the investigator, Dustin wasn't working. He probably thought he could get the decision reversed and the Marines would take him back."

"Doesn't hurt to swing by his ex-wife's place." He turned the key, put the truck in gear, and steered onto the two-lane road. "Enter the address into my phone and see if there's a drive-thru along the way."

Thirty minutes later, with a bag full of double-bacon cheeseburgers and fries between them, he parked across the street and two doors down from a split-level ranch. An American flag hung beside the front door. Flower beds separated the neatly mowed front lawn from the house. And a man stood in the center of the trimmed grass holding a baseball.

He was a big guy, with a build that suggested he could have played football if he lost the beer belly. A boy of eight or maybe nine waited on the far side with his glove.

"Mom's going to be mad that you let me play catch when I'm sick," the child called out.

"Looks like you're feeling better now," the man said with a laugh. "And the fresh air is good for you. Ask any doctor."

"Oh my God." The faint whisper filled the cab of the truck tearing Josh's focus from the all-American family scene outside.

"Caroline?"

"That's him," she murmured. "That's Dustin. And he's . . . he's playing ball. After everything . . ."

A familiar rage pulsed through him. If he let go, he'd climb out of the truck and attack that bastard. He'd—

"He went back to his family. His wife and kids. He went back as if . . . as if nothing happened," she murmured.

"Why don't I go and talk to him?" Josh said. *And we'll have another date after you bail me out of jail.*

He knew she couldn't walk into a police station. But spending a night or two behind bars before his brothers came for him seemed a small price to pay.

"No," she said firmly. "Just drive. *Please.*"

And this time it wasn't a command masquerading as a plea. She was close to begging. With one last look at the bastard who'd stripped away her security, who'd made her feel like she needed to be fucking less—less beautiful, less bold, less brave—he turned the key and revved the engine.

Dustin looked over, his brow furrowed in fucking concern as Josh peeled out of the parking space.

About time you worried about something, Josh thought.

The bastard couldn't see them. Not with the midday sun high in the sky and the dark tint on Josh's truck windows. Logic told him that was a damn good thing. He didn't want her former CO coming after them. But the other part of him wanted to send a message to Dustin.

She hasn't forgotten, asshole.

And now she had a whole team, or whatever the hell they called it in the Marines, on her side. She had him. She had Noah, Josie, and the rest of the staff at Big Buck's. And she had his brothers and his sister on her side. Even if they didn't know her full story, they'd fight for her. She was family. She was *his*, dammit. Not to possess, but to love and protect with everything he had.

"Where do you want to go?" he said as they turned the corner and the all-American rapist disappeared from sight. He wanted to get her away from here and find a place where he could take care of her.

"The beach," she murmured. "Take me back to the ocean."

"As you wish, Caroline." He headed for the highway, determined to put a few miles between them and the man who'd managed to do what Caroline couldn't—move forward.

Chapter 13

CAROLINE BURIED HER toes in the sand. Then she waited
for a wave to rush up and sweep the fine white grains
back to sea. But the tide had already receded and her feet
remained buried. Still, the chill from the rushing waves
ran upward from her feet to her calves. She'd rolled up
her cargo pants and removed her boots. She'd needed to
feel something other than shock and sadness.

*If I stay here long enough I'll freeze and break into
pieces,* she thought. *But at least then I won't have to run
anymore. To live in hiding while he plays ball with his
kids.*

Seeing Dustin hadn't delivered a neatly wrapped box
full of closure. She'd been naïve to believe driving down
here would lock her past away where it belonged. And she
knew that she couldn't stop running unless she turned
herself in to the military.

Five hours sitting on the beach, watching the waves

and noting the tide, delivered a hefty dose of clarity along with the chill.

And Josh.

He'd offered a strong, determined presence seemingly at odds with his charming smile. Along with the burger he'd set on her lap and told her to eat, he'd secured rooms for them at an oceanfront motel. It wasn't the Oregon cottage, but seeing as she'd spent most of the day sitting on the motel's beach, it felt like the right choice.

So had leaving the Marines, the branch of the military that she'd wanted to join since she was a kid. And standing up in military court and telling the truth about her CO. All good, solid choices.

Yet she was the one who'd spent the past year hiding and constantly looking over her shoulder. She'd been terrified to live her life.

But not Dustin. He'd picked up the pieces and moved on.

The injustice turned her stomach. And for a moment, she felt as if she would throw up the burger.

"Are you cold?" Josh settled in the sand next to her and held out a Moore Timber sweatshirt.

"Yes," she said, taking the extra layer and pulling it over her plain black T-shirt.

"I'm guessing that wasn't what you were expecting to find," he said.

She turned away from the water and looked at him. He still wore the same jeans and long-sleeve flannel shirt. But he'd traded his boots for a pair of flip-flops.

"No," she said slowly. "I had this picture in my head

that he would be sitting in his rented apartment alone. Maybe drinking a beer in the middle of the morning."

"I'm guessing he didn't have the beer gut when he served," Josh said.

She shook her head. "Yeah, that's something. But I still can't believe his wife took him back."

"You don't know that full story. I've been thinking about this since we left. A sick kid, home from school while the mom needs to work. Maybe she called and demanded that he come over."

"Maybe," she said. But Dustin had appeared at ease, at home on the picture-perfect lawn.

Josh looked down at his feet. "You know how I told you my mom left when I was a kid?"

She nodded.

"It happened just like that," he said. "One day she just walked out the door. My father was back from flying choppers for the army and I don't know, but I guess she decided she'd had enough of taking care of four kids on next to nothing.

"I'll never know why she left." He looked up and met her gaze. "Once or twice I thought about trying to find her. I wondered if hearing her side of the story would bring, I don't know—"

"Closure," she supplied.

"Yeah. And look, I know it's not the same. Dustin attacked you. What he did . . ."

Josh pressed his lips together and a ripple of tension moved down his arms. The muscles in his forearms looked ready to jump into action.

"It makes me want to hit something too," she said. "But you're right. Looking back won't help me get my life back on track. If he had been sitting around drunk and feeling sorry for himself in the middle of the morning, that wouldn't have erased the past."

"Nothing will," he said. "But that doesn't mean you can't look ahead and try to rebuild your life."

"And if I can't?" she whispered, hating the hollow sound of fear in her soft words.

He reached over and took her hand. "I wonder that same thing all the time. I survived a week in a coma and lived. I lost my memory and got it back. Life gave me another shot. What if it amounts to nothing? What if I waste it?"

"You have a plan," she pointed out. "The big house on a nice piece of land."

"I do. And it's a good one." He reached over and took her hand, interlacing his fingers with hers. "But if I had to choose between eating cold fries out here on the beach with you and the vision of domestic bliss I've mapped out in my imagination, I'd stay right here."

"Josh," she murmured.

He offered her a smile. "I'd rather have another date with you."

I believe you and your cocky, too-charming grin. I'm halfway in love with it. . .

If she let herself walk into the future and claim Josh Summers, she just might fall for him completely.

But loving Josh didn't cancel out her past. And it wouldn't change the fact that she was still being hunted. Not by Dustin. No, today had made that crystal clear. Dustin wasn't biding his time until he could seek his revenge.

She was being hounded by her own choices—to run, to hide, and to live in fear of taking another shot at a life. It was time to make better decisions. And it was time to listen to her heart instead of giving her fear free rein.

He gave her hand a squeeze. "This doesn't have to be date. We could swap foot rubs on the beach instead of back massages and then go to our separate rooms."

"Is that what you want?" she asked. If she pushed past her reservations, if she listened to her desire, she wanted a fourth date. But maybe today—and seeing the man who'd raped her—had shaken him. What had happened in Afghanistan had always been very real to her. Maybe today had shifted her past from a word or concept into a tangible thing for him too. "You would rather have me rub your feet instead of—"

"No," he said firmly. But he pulled his hand free from hers. He ran his fingers through his red curls. "That's not it, Caroline. There isn't a part of my body that I don't want you to touch."

She leaned back and rested her palms on the sand. "If you think I won't take you up on that offer," she said in a no-nonsense tone, "then I'm afraid I'm going to insist on another date."

His smile faded, but he kept his gaze fixed on her, his expression open and sincere. "Caroline, I need you to go to bed with me because you want *me*. If tonight, after our adventure today, you're looking for a way to move on, then we'll wait."

Relief rushed in. She tipped her chin to her chest and grinned. Josh held tight to what he needed. No guessing. No games. Now it was her turn.

"When I was touching you last night, the feel of your shoulder blades turned me on." She looked up at him. "You sat in a hospital for month, yet now every inch of you is perfect. And don't tell me it's from baking."

"I spend most days holding a chainsaw, not a spatula," he pointed out, a hint of his smile returning.

"I felt the strength in your muscles and I wasn't afraid you would overpower me—"

"Never," he said firmly.

"I know." She sat up, pulling her hands free from the sand. And she reached for him. Her fingers brushed the coarse stubble on his cheeks. He hadn't bothered to shave this morning. Now he looked a little rough and so sexy she wondered for a moment why he'd stayed. He'd waited a long time for her. And he was willing to keep their relationship out of the bedroom a while longer.

She searched for the right words. "You feel good. All of you. Your shoulders, your lower back, your kisses . . ." She leaned close and pressed her lips to his. Fighting the urge to linger and explore, she drew back. "And your company. You feel right and good. And I'm not saying this to seduce you—"

"Just to boost my ego?" he said.

"Just take me at my word," she murmured. "You feel like an impending orgasm."

CAROLINE HAD NEVER lied to him. Not even that first night when he'd found her camped out. Sure, she'd withheld details. But that just proved she wasn't stupid. No one shared their life story, their personal tragedies, or even their last name, with a stranger they met in the woods.

So if she said touching him, hell, even sharing the same section of beach with him, pushed her close to the big O, he believed her.

"Are you ready?" He reached for her. Placing his hands on her hips, he drew her closer. And she came willingly, shifting to her side and then climbing onto his lap. Her legs straddled his and her knees pressed into the sand straddling his thighs.

"For hours of naughty foreplay *after* our dinner date?" she asked, running her hands over his supposedly orgasm-worthy shoulders.

He laughed. And after the wound-up, fucked-up day they'd shared, it felt good. "You're hungry again?" He ran his hand up her thighs and pictured stripping off her cargo pants. He wanted to feel her bare skin. "I brought you a lukewarm burger."

"Hours ago. Plus, this is a date."

"Hmm." His fingers roamed over her hips, shifting higher and higher. He pressed the heel of his hand against her lower back and drew her closer. "I meant are you ready for those dirty words I promised you? I vote we skip dinner and kick off the foreplay with another showing of your underwear."

She arched beneath his touch and then rocked her hips forward. Even though she'd given him one helluva green light, he didn't thrust up to meet her. He let her set the motion, moving over his erection as if she also wished their clothes would magically disappear.

"Are you sure we shouldn't wait?" she asked. "We could go back to the room and order room service. My treat. Talk some more . . ."

"If you keep moving like that, I won't make it until we get back to the room." His lips hovered over her neck. He punctuated the statement with a kiss to the soft skin just above her shoulder.

She leaned back and her hips stilled. And his dick throbbed, demanding that he voice an objection. But her gaze was fixed on a point over his shoulder.

"I'm not sure this place offers room service," she said.

"We'll order pizza. Later." He wrapped his left arm around her. His right hand pressed into the sand seeking leverage. "Now, hold on tight."

He pushed off the beach, but managed to keep her strong, petite body wrapped around his. Her thighs pressed tight against his sides.

So damn strong, he thought. She could hold on to him without his help, but he palmed her butt anyway, carrying her toward the motel with one firm cheek resting in each hand.

He saw an older couple, probably twenty years their senior, ahead of them on the path. He strode past them and offered a friendly greeting. And Caroline buried her face against his neck.

"Hiding?" he asked once they were out of earshot.

"Something like that." She ran her tongue down the V-neckline of his button-down shirt. "Or maybe I just wanted a taste," she added, her lips moving against his skin as she spoke.

"It's a damn good thing our rooms are on the first floor with an ocean view," he growled.

He reached the door and reluctantly lowered her to the ground. As soon as her feet touched the pavement, he missed the warmth of her body against his.

"So here's the thing," he said, withdrawing the room key, an old-fashioned actual key on a ring, from his pocket. "I think we need to work our way up to pizza. Get good and hungry first."

"A date in reverse? Start in bed and go backward?"

"Yeah, and later we can blame my memory. I still struggle with sequences," he said. "Sometimes I add the baking soda before the eggs. But don't worry, I never forget to preheat the oven."

"I don't know." She looked up at him. "It could take up to thirty minutes for delivery . . . but if you think you'll need more time."

I don't think I'll last five minutes, he thought.

But he nodded. When they got inside, he would take a step back and remind himself to slow the hell down. The key turned and the locked clicked. He pushed the door open and held it for her.

As soon as it clicked shut behind them, she disappeared behind him. "Caroline?"

"Don't mind me," she murmured. He could feel her

breath on his neck. "I'm just going to help you out of your shirt. And while I work your buttons . . ." She released the third one, extending the V of his neckline to the middle of his chest. He'd forgotten to pack an undershirt, but he'd tossed in a box of condoms just in case.

"You can tell me all of the naughty things you want to do to me after I get you out of these clothes. How you like to be touched—" She'd released another two buttons and paused to slide her hands inside his open shirt, running her hands over his lower ribs. "Where you want my mouth . . ."

Her fingers moved to the top of his jeans and he groaned. But he caught hold of her wrists before she lowered his zipper and reached inside. "Shouldn't I be the one asking the questions?" she asked.

She pulled away and he instantly released her.

"Sorry," he said. Shit, he didn't want to apologize for wanting to give her what she'd asked for. He had to do this right. "But I don't want to frighten you. I need to know how to touch you, what you like—"

"Josh." She moved around to stand in front of him again. But she didn't reach for him. "Do I look scared?"

He ran his hands through his hair. "I meant I don't want to do something that would trigger a reaction."

"Then we better keep our clothes on and order pizza. Because when I said you look like an impending orgasm, I didn't mean I would come from staring at you. I'm hoping you'll make love to me until you trigger a reaction so big that I'm begging you for another the minute it subsides."

"Caroline, I'm trying to be careful."

"Well, stop," she shot back. "You've never treated me like I might break apart at any second. Please don't start now."

He studied the fierce woman who'd been undressing him until he threw on the brakes. She was right. If he trusted her, he didn't need to question his every move. She'd speak up for herself.

"All right."

She stepped closer, but still didn't touch him. Her chin high, her green eyes flashing with a combination of desire and determination, she stared up at him.

"Talk to me. Touch me," she said as her fingers curled around the edge of her black T-shirt. Then she drew it over her head. She tossed it aside and reached behind her to free her bra. "Don't hold back."

Josh kissed his restraint goodbye and placed his hands on her bare chest. The weight settled into his palms. Her nipples formed tight peaks as he lifted and pressed her breasts together. He hunched his shoulders and lowered his mouth to her skin. And his tongue dipped into her cleavage.

Her fingers worked into his hair, holding him close. "Josh, for the record, I love the way you use your mouth."

Love.

It was too soon to tell her he was falling for a helluva lot more than her mouth. No, he still needed to prove that this—his lips exploring her body—worked for them.

He pressed one more kiss to her breasts. Then he released her chest and lowered down to his knees. And he reached for her steel-toed boots.

"First I'm going to get you out of these ass-kicking shoes." His fingers worked the laces. "And then I want another look at your panties before I slide them down your legs and show you exactly what I can do with my mouth."

Chapter 14

JOSH SUMMERS HAD turned stripping off her socks into foreplay. She'd never thought of her ankles as an erogenous zone. But when he touched them, she'd felt a rush of heat and need settle beneath her black lace undies. Then the feel of his fingers against her skin as he unbuttoned her pants and drew down the zipper had pushed her so close to a climax that he might as well have been vibrating.

Now her boots rested at the foot of the motel's queen-sized bed. Her cargo pants lay discarded in a heap beside them. She'd lost everything but her panties. She looked down at the man kneeling at her feet. He'd tossed aside his shirt and pants too, but kept his underwear. His head was cocked to one side, and his gaze fixed on her last piece of clothing.

"Not complicated," she murmured. "Just grab ahold of the top and pull them down."

Don't mind me, she thought. *I might come before you get them off.*

"Hmm." He ran his hands up her calves, over her knees, and paused at her thighs. Then he leaned forward, captured the top of her panties between his teeth, and drew them down to her thighs. "Like that?"

Oh God, yes!

But she went with a swift, sharp nod. Not that he could see her affirmative gesture. His gaze remained focused on the dark curls between her legs as he drew her underwear down her legs. She stepped out of them before he asked and the slip of black lace joined her pants on the floor.

"Place your foot on my shoulder," he said.

She allowed him to guide her left foot into a position that left her knee raised practically to her chest. Balancing precariously on her other foot, she felt open, exposed, and ready—for a physically impracticable event.

Kneeling in front of her five foot five frame, his mouth was level with her chest, not her . . .

"Impossible," she murmured.

"No, Caroline." He looked up at her with his trust-me grin. "This will work. Believe me."

And here, in this room, when it came to pleasure and sex, she had faith in him.

With his hand on her right hip holding her steady, he sat back on his heels and brushed his tongue over her bare flesh. She ran her hands through his hair and held on hoping she wouldn't fall away from . . .

Oh my . . . goodness. . .

Josh had offered to give her a demonstration of just

what he could do with his mouth and wow had he delivered. She closed her eyes and narrowed her focus to his tongue. Pleasure rippled through her like the waves she'd watched earlier. And it overrode her other emotions.

She pulled on his hair, silently begging for more. More pressure. More teasing, tantalizing stokes designed to turn her legs into a trembling mess . . .

He read her mind and gave it to her.

She'd been a fool to wait for this. For over a year, this man had been bringing her pies, brownies, and cupcakes. But if she'd let down her guard, if she'd agreed to go out with him before now . . .

Later, much later, she would have a moment of silence for all of the orgasms she'd missed out on because she'd been too afraid to fall for this man.

"This is so much better than pie," she groaned.

He chuckled as he drew his mouth away. "Even the pecan?"

"Yes." Her fingers still woven through his curls, she tugged his head back into position and he complied.

Another lick . . .

"Oh wow, that's better than key lime with homemade . . ." She moaned. "Whipped . . . *oh God* . . . cream! Yes!"

"Next time I make 'oh God cream,'" he murmured, his mouth still oh-so-close to the most needy, intimate parts of her body, "I'll cover you in homemade topping." He stole a lick, then added: "With a cherry on top."

"Not another dirty word out of you until you make me come," she said.

He laughed again. But there was nothing cruel about the sound. Not this time. Not here. Not with this man.

She tensed for the rush of memory. Another man. In another place. Laughing *at* her, not with her. Promising pleasure she didn't want. And delivering fear. So much fear she'd lived and breathed it for months. She'd let it rule her life. All because of that bastard.

"Caroline?" the man kneeling in a seemingly impossible position at her feet asked softly.

She pushed the memories away. They wouldn't disappear. What Dustin had done to her, how much he'd taken from her . . . the invisible scars would fade but never disappear.

But they were no longer immobile barriers to her future.

"OK, maybe one or two more naughty images," she said, wanting to hear his voice while the hand not holding her hip steady explored and stroked her.

"You know, I'm willing to share my whipped cream," he murmured. "Anytime you want a taste, you can rub some over my chest—"

"Just your chest?" she challenged.

"Use your imagination. My dirty mouth has some unfinished business."

And then he buried his head between her legs again. She closed her eyes and let the sensations hold her right here, in this moment. His tongue drew tight circles around the bundle of nerves primed by his words and his touch to send her falling . . .

"Josh," she whispered. "Josh."

She repeated his name, over and over as she came bucking against his face, accepting all he had to offer.

AFTER HIS ACCIDENT, if someone had told Josh that he'd get a second shot at the life he wanted while crouched on the floor of a motel in Eureka, he would have called them crazy. But right now, listening to the woman he loved call out his name over and over, he knew he'd found what he'd been looking for. He didn't need the big house nestled in the valley, or the fancy kitchen . . .

Just Caroline.

"Josh?" she murmured. And it was no longer an *oh more, more, more, Josh,* but a question.

He drew his mouth away from her and looked up.

"We need to move to the bed or the floor," she said, her eyes still glazed over with pleasure. "Your choice. But I can't maintain this position any longer."

"The bed," he decided as he placed his hand on her left foot and gently lowered it from his shoulder to the floor. But he kept ahold of her hip. As he rose up from the ground, his free hand reached for her. His fingers pressed into her backside. Using his firm grip on her hips, he guided her toward the bed, turning her until she lined up with the queen-sized mattress.

"Lie down," he murmured, releasing her. "I'll be right back."

He rushed over to his duffel bag and rummaged through it until he found the box of condoms. He tore open the packaging and pulled one out.

And realized he was still wearing his freaking under-wear.

"Josh?" she called from the bed.

He glanced over his shoulder.

"I want to watch this part," she said.

"Yeah?" he arched an eyebrow as he turned and walked over to the bed. He tossed the condom onto the comforter and hooked his thumbs under the elastic band. Slowly, he drew down his last article of clothing. Her lips parted as he revealed his aching, eager dick.

"Next time, I'll do a striptease worthy of *Magic Mike*." He pulled his underwear down his legs and stepped out of them.

"I don't need a dance," she said. "You. I just want you."

"You've got me." He reached for the condom.

"You know," she began. And his hand froze, holding the unwrapped condom over the head of his cock. "I might need you to paint me a picture of what you want."

Paint her a picture?

But his brain kicked back into gear, and he searched for the right words.

"Caroline." He covered himself and walked back to the foot of the bed. "I want you."

He climbed up on the bed, his knees pushing into the mattress between her legs as he covered her body with his own. His elbows rested close to her shoulders, holding his weight off her body. "I've wanted you for so damn long. And I swear, I'll tell you everything I've imagined. How. Where. But right now . . . right now just know that it is all with you. You're my fantasy."

"Yes," she said with a soft laugh.

She reached between them and wrapped her hand around his cock. She drew him closer to where he needed to be as her legs wound around him.

"Now?" he murmured.

"Now," she confirmed.

He pushed past her hand and slid inside her. He'd thought about this moment, moved through it in his dreams. He'd tried to prepare for each stroke and anticipate her reaction. He'd wanted to be ready . . .

And now he let it all go. He had faith in her. She'd tell him if she needed more, less, a different position . . .

He thrust into her again and again, holding nothing back. And she moved with him. Her body rocked up to greet him, opening to him. He didn't worry about hurting her or taking her too hard or fast. She was taking him right back, consuming him.

Her nails dug into his back as she arched beneath him. He wasn't lost in pleasure. He was right freaking here in their Eureka motel room, making love to her. This was it, what he'd been searching for. He'd found what he wanted. And he was all in, no holding back. No matter what the future brought them. She was *his*. And he'd hold on to her, love her, care for her with all his heart.

"Caroline," he roared. Then he lowered his mouth to hers and claimed her lips, kissing her as the climax ripped through him.

I love you.

Now, buried inside her, wasn't the time to say the words out loud. Soon. But not now.

Chapter 15

CAROLINE STARED AT the brick pathway leading to the yellow colonial. Long, white columns stretched the full two stories of the impressive home. The house had wings, stretching from either side. They could easily fit Noah's three-bedroom farmhouse in this mansion and probably the barn too. Though they might want to leave the old mechanical bull on the front lawn to annoy the neighbors. But that would ruin the mansion's equally impressive landscaping.

Manicured hedges lined the brick path leading from the sidewalk to the front entrance. On the right, a paved driveway wound around the side of the house. Trimmed grass filled the space between the bushes and the pavement. A glimpse of a stone pathway leading to a garden was visible around the left of the home.

"Ready to get out?" Josh asked. "The guard at the gate called up. She knows we're here."

Caroline nodded and reached for her door. "We should have made a plan on the drive."

Instead of talking about what they would say now that they'd finally arrived at the end of their road trip, she'd spent the drive down from Eureka staring out the window. She'd made love to Josh Summers last night. After all this time, she'd gone to bed with him. She'd spent the night curled around his strong, powerful body. And she'd woken up with her head resting on the red-gold hair covering his chest.

She'd blown past impossible, pushed failure aside, and claimed her second chance. And now she didn't want to let go. She wanted to hold on to him with all her heart.

But she'd fallen for a man who didn't lie. He refused to pretend. Meanwhile she was afraid to use her real name. One glorious, orgasm-filled night didn't erase the federal warrant hanging over her head.

Josh appeared at her side as her feet touched down on the sidewalk. "Ready?"

The white front door swung open and Helena waved down at them, a smile plastered on her face.

"She looks happy to see us." Josh grinned and raised his free hand.

"Appearances can be deceiving."

But he drew her forward, leading her down the brick path. Halfway to the front door, he inclined his head toward hers. "Say what you wish someone had said to you."

"Chop off his balls?" she muttered.

"That seems a little extreme if we're wrong and her

husband's just a giant ass who likes to yell at his wife," he said.

"True."

They reached the front steps and turned their attention to the woman who looked about as manicured as her hedges. There wasn't a strand of hair out of place on her blond bob. Her pale pink dress screamed 'designer.' And her peep-toe white patent leather heels made Caroline's combat boots look decidedly out of place. But who wore heels in their own home?

"Hello," Caroline said.

"What are you doing here?" Helena hissed through her smiling teeth once they'd reached the top of the brick steps leading to the front door. "Are you crazy? I can't believe you *followed me home* after eavesdropping on one little phone call!"

Josh drew Caroline closer to his side. "We were in Northern Cali anyway—"

"My husband will be back soon," Helena snapped, her smile fading now. She looked close to tears again. "I'd like you to leave. *Please.*"

"Your friends were concerned," Josh started. But she'd already stepped back and closed the door.

Caroline stared at the brass knocker and debated trying again. But if Helena didn't want them here, what more could they do?

"I guess you should have replaced 'hello' with 'cut off his balls,'" Josh said. "Want to try again?"

She shook her head. "Let's go. We can have Lily call and see if she can convince Helena to meet with us at a bar or restaurant. Or at our hotel if Helena would prefer someplace more private. Even if she agrees to meet with us, all we can do is offer help. We can't force her to leave. We can listen. But we can't save her. She needs to make that call on her own."

"We're hanging up our superhero capes?" he said as they reached his truck.

"She needs to be her own hero." Caroline opened the passenger door and climbed into the truck. "We came down here so that she knows someone is here for her. There's a way out if she wants it."

But the escape route comes with its own pitfalls.

Caroline glanced back at the house. She'd fought back, but she wasn't free. Not yet. And the only way to get there?

No, she pushed that thought aside. Turning herself in wouldn't set her free. She'd be locked up in a military jail.

"It's past lunch time," Josh pointed out.

"And we need to find a place to stay," she said.

Josh picked up his phone and asked SIRI for directions to the nearest hotel.

"You forgot cheapest," she pointed out once the phone offered an address.

"This doesn't look like the cheap part of town," he said as they pulled through the security gates at the front of the community. "If you want Helena to visit us, we can't expect her to drive an hour away."

"I only have so much cash," she said. *And no access to bank accounts or credit cards.*

"This is technically our fifth date. My turn to pick the location and pay."

"You paid for the motel last night too," she pointed out.

"Extenuating circumstances. We were already right there."

That was one way to look at her meltdown on the beach yesterday. But so far he'd paid for everything on their road trip—a trip that had been her idea from the beginning. Of course without him, she would have had to have relied on Noah or Josie to purchase a bus ticket for her. Hiking would have taken too long—especially for their anxious friend in the air force.

"I'll pay you back for the rooms last night," she said.

He shook his head. "Just have your golden lasso ready."

WHILE JOSH WENT out to pick up a pizza instead of splurging on the overpriced room service, Caroline surveyed the five-star room for something that resembled Wonder Woman's lasso. His cell phone's not-so-budget-friendly selection featured a queen-sized bed. The modern headboard and nightstands were permanently attached to the wall. Not far from the foot of the bed stood an oval-shaped desk with a sleek black chair. Beside the desk was a cabinet that housed a flat-screen television and the mini-fridge, but sadly lacked a golden lasso.

She walked through the bathroom. Shower. Tub. Two sinks. A stack of white towels that might work if she cut them apart . . . But she moved on to the closet.

And after careful consideration she selected the white sash from one of the bathrobes provided by the hotel. She set the sash on the bed. She could do this. She could play the part of the superhero seductress.

"I have pizza," Josh called. The smell of melted cheese followed him into the room. "I also talked to Lily. She promised to text Helena's number. We can try calling later. Maybe her husband will be out? Or in bed already?"

"Maybe." She picked up the sash and dangled it in the air between them. "I found my lasso while you were out. How hungry are you?"

"For half a pie? I need a workout first." He set the pizza on the table and headed for the bed. He pulled off his Moore Timber T-shirt as he moved past her and tossed it aside.

"I think we'll work up an appetite." She toyed with the makeshift lasso, pulling it taut between her hands.

He sat on the edge of the bed and held out his hands. "I'm ready for your best superhero impression."

"Oh no, this is your date. You call the shots," she said.

"You want me to tell you how I like to be tied up?" he said with a laugh.

She nodded as anticipation spread through her, honing in on the part of her body most likely to respond to his touch.

"All right." He stood up and began stripping off his jeans. "First thing, I'll need you to lose the clothes."

"Ah, the 'get naked' step." She pulled off her top. Her cargo pants joined her boots, shirt, and underwear in a pile. "You know, so many of the comic books skip that step."

"It's a shame." He kicked off his boxers and they flew

across the room. "Now I want you to tie one end of the rope around my wrist." He held out a hand. "And the other to yours."

"Worried I'll run away?" she teased as she followed his instructions. She tied a double knot at each end, but struggled with her wrist.

"This way I'll be able to rein you in if you get too wild," he said as he took the end of the rope from her and finished binding her left wrist to his right.

"I wasn't planning to go far." She sank to her knees and ran her hands up his thighs. Unlike his position last night, her mouth lined up perfectly with his erection.

"Fuck," he murmured.

"Soon. Very soon. But first . . ." She wrapped her hand around him and guided him to her lips. Pumping her hand up and down his hard, thick length, she ran her tongue around the tip of his cock.

"Caroline," he gasped.

There was a power that accompanied giving him pleasure and hearing him call her name as her mouth moved over him. Her free hand—unbound and not working his cock—reached for his ass. The muscles tensed beneath her touch as his hips rocked forward into her mouth.

"Too much?" he murmured, pulling back.

She ran her lips up and released him. "Trust me. I'll tell you."

"I do." His fingers worked their way into her hair, drawing her mouth back to his erection. "Trust you, that is. But I have limits too. Lick me. Suck on me. But I want to come inside you."

Her hand rose up to meet her lips and he pulled away. Still tied to him, she dropped to all fours and crawled after him . . .

He glanced behind him. "Shit. I forgot," he said, eyes widened, before he turned back to his bag and retrieved a condom. She heard the rip and felt the tug on the tie holding them together as he covered himself. Then he looked over his shoulder. "To the bed?"

She nodded and rose up onto her knees. She placed her hands on his butt and held on as she shifted to her feet. "Work on your glutes while baking those pies?"

"You have no idea," he said with a bark of laughter.

She stepped away and pulled on the sash. "This time, I want to ride you."

He turned and backed up to the foot of the bed. Slowly, he sat down. "Ready?"

She nodded. And he leaned back on the mattress. She moved with him, climbing onto him, her legs straddling his thighs. She inched her way forward, her hands pressing into his chest as she rose up and then sank down onto his cock.

She welcomed the control. But more than anything, as she began to rock her hips, she wanted his pleasure. She wanted to push him over the edge and fall with him. She felt free, riding him closer and closer to the peak of pleasure—even while bound to him.

Somehow, I'll find a way to make this work. I'll find a way to stay with him.

Chapter 16

CAROLINE PICKED UP the hotel phone at nine-thirty that evening and dialed the number Lily had sent to Josh's cell. They'd tried once earlier—after they'd shared a shower and pizza—but they'd reached Helena and Ashford's answering machine.

"Hello?" a soft, female voice said.

Her pulse quickened. "Helena? Please don't hang up," she said quickly as Josh sat down on the bed next to her. "This is Caroline. We met on your trip to Forever and I stopped by today with Josh Summers. We'd like to meet with you. Sit down and talk to you. At our hotel or—"

"I can't come meet you," Helena whispered urgently. "Not tonight."

Josh leaned in to hear and she tilted the phone. "What about tomorrow?" she asked as footsteps sounded in the background. "I just want to offer you a way out if you want it. Someone to talk to—"

"Why?"

Her voice was so low that Caroline almost missed the word. "Because your friend, Noah Tager, he was there for me when I needed help. He stood up for me. He tried to save me. And as soon as I knew I wasn't alone . . . I fought back."

Caroline closed her eyes. She could still picture the first time Noah had fallen in step beside her while she walked across the base. At first she'd thought she'd misjudged him. He'd seemed like one of the good guys and now she'd have to fight him off too. And probably lose given his tall, muscular frame. He'd win, just like Dustin had won, even if she fought.

But then Noah had stopped by the bathroom door and murmured *I'll walk you back when you're done. He won't get to you while I'm standing here.*

"You're not alone," Caroline said to the woman on the other line.

"You can't help me."

The whisper shot through the phone and Caroline's stomach dropped. "Just don't hang up," she said. "Please, Helena."

"Who are you talking to?" a man's deep baritone asked. He didn't raise his voice. But he didn't need to. The sound carried. And Caroline recognized the implied threat in his seemingly harmless words.

"Someone from the club," Helena answered quickly. "About a tennis match."

Oh no, lies are never a good sign. . . .

"At nine-thirty at night?" he said.

"An emergency," Helena called, her voice slightly muffled as if she'd partially covered the receiver.

"Who is it?" he asked, his tone low and threaded with steel. "Who are you talking to?"

Helena hesitated. Caroline heard the unsteady hiss of breath and she knew the woman on the other end of the line had waited too long.

"Hang up." The man's words were barely audible through the phone.

"Yes," Helena said. And then, "I'm sorry, I—"

"Hang up," he barked.

Caroline waited for the line to go dead, her chest rising and falling with one trembling breath after another. Tension rippled through her. But instead she heard a shuffling. A tap as if the phone had been dropped, or maybe placed somewhere?

She looked over at Josh. His brow was furrowed and his expression focused. He glanced over at her and mouthed the words *we listen*.

But Caroline wasn't sure she wanted to hear what came next. What if—

"Get on the bed," the deep male voice said.

Caroline covered the receiver. If they weren't silent, they would give her away. And if Helena had been trying to prove a point, if she wanted to show them once and for all that her husband wasn't hurting her, then they might be here for a while. But if she was reaching out and asking for help . . .

A chill ran down her spine. She realized that being able to empathize with Helena didn't necessarily make her the best person for this mission. But they were here now and they would find a way to deliver whatever she needed.

"I'll be right there," Helena called, her tone bright and cheerful.

Caroline drew her lower lip between her teeth. If they'd made a mistake coming down here—

"Now!" The male voice—presumably Helena's husband—boomed through the hotel receiver.

And Caroline jumped, nearly dropping the phone. Josh wrapped his arm around her and held her to his side. The phone remained between them, cradled in her grasp. She heard footsteps, followed by a rustling. Sheets? Discarded clothes?

And then a soft moan.

"No, Ash," Helena murmured. "Not right now. I'm not ready."

"You don't say no," he growled. Ashford—her husband—Caroline thought as she mentally assigned the name to the baritone.

"Please," Helena said. "Just let me—"

"You don't say no, baby. Not to me," her husband said. "Now lie down on the bed."

He's going to rape her. Right now. While we listen. . .

It didn't matter that he was her husband. The fact that Helena had trusted him once upon a time only made it worse. She'd made promises to him.

But that doesn't strip away her right to say no.

"I'm calling the police," Josh murmured, his voice a low growl. He stood and withdrew his cell from the front pocket of his jeans. He moved toward the bathroom and stepped inside to place the call. But he kept the door open and his gaze fixed on her.

Josh returned, his cell in hand, and leaned down to her ear. "The police are on their way. We should meet them. They will need our statements."

She nodded. But she knew the cops would require more than that. She's seen the size of Ashford's house. They would need proof if Helena had any hope of breaking free from a man like that. And Caroline guessed Helena had known that from the beginning. She couldn't run from her husband. Helena had to fight. And for that, she needed hard evidence.

She grabbed Josh's phone and pressed buttons until she found the one she needed.

Record.

JOSH GLANCED AT the clock on the nightstand. A matter of minutes had passed since he'd hung up with the local cops, but they had to go soon and meet the police. Shit, he wanted to leave Caroline behind, but he would need help getting Helena away from that place. And he didn't want Caroline to be alone.

Talk about a trigger. This one is a fucking nightmare.

If he'd known their little road trip would end with them listening to a woman's husband taking her against her will, he would have demanded that Noah, Dominic—anyone else—go on this mission. He'd honestly thought they'd get here, hit the roadblock they'd met today—

Helena turning them away at the door—and head back to Forever.

"Caroline?" he murmured. He ran his hand down her arm and took his cell. The sounds on the other line had stopped. He ended the recording, pocketed the phone, and reached for her hand. "We need to go."

"OK." She stood and took his hand. And then glanced at her backpack, resting beside the hotel bed. "I should get my—"

"No guns," he said. "We called in the cavalry. Let them bring the firepower. We don't want questions about permits that we can't answer."

"You're right," she said slowly. "But I could bring the bag and leave it in the car. Just in case."

"No." He drew her toward the door. "Trust me on this."

He led her to the elevator bank and down to the garage where they'd parked his truck. Guiding her into the passenger seat, he fastened her belt. Then he climbed in and drove as fast as he could to Helena's gated community. He offered the wide-eyed night security guard a rushed explanation. But as soon as he said he was with the cops, the guard waved them through.

"Wait here," Josh said as they pulled up in front. The lights were on in the entry and he saw Ashford standing in the doorway talking to a pair of uniformed policemen.

One look and Josh wanted to take aim at Asshole Ashford's face. He wanted to leave bloodstains on the man's silk bathrobe. Helena's husband probably worked out. There had to be a gym somewhere in his enormous house. But Josh could still take him.

Right here on your freaking perfect lawn, asshole.

He approached the front door. "Evening, officers. Josh Summers. I'm the one who placed the call."

"My wife's not home tonight," Ashford said sharply. "I don't know what kind of prank you're trying to pull here, but I'll say good-night now."

Ashford moved to close the door, but Josh said, "I don't think so."

He held out his phone and pressed play on the recording. Helena's pleading filled the quiet.

"Where did you get that?" Ashford demanded.

The officers' eyes widened at the man in the bathrobe that probably cost half their salary. And Josh looked too, just in time to see a fist swing at his face.

Chapter 17

CAROLINE TRANSLATED *WAIT in the truck* to *stay here until someone starts throwing punches.* She saw Josh dodge the blow as she slammed the passenger door. She raced over the manicured lawn and leaped over the hedges.

By the time the policemen grabbed Ashford and hauled the bastard's arms behind his back, she'd reached the front door. She kept going. She heard one officer reciting the Miranda rights while the other radioed for backup.

Why the hell aren't they looking for Helena?

That jerk belonged in jail. But it didn't end there. Not for Helena.

"Helena!" Caroline called into the house. "Helena!"

Helena rushed into the foyer and Caroline froze. She blinked, taking in Helena's wild mane of blond hair. She'd traded her pretty pink dress from this afternoon for a pair of silk pajama bottoms and a black tank top. And she'd traded her heels for tennis shoes. She had a purse slung over her shoulder as if ready to make a break for it with or without the police presence.

"You came," Helena said, rushing into the marble entryway.

Caroline caught the other woman in her arms and felt her break. With her face pressed against Caroline's shoulder, Helena wept. She wrapped her arms around Caroline and held on tight.

"We're going to get you out of here," Caroline murmured. "We'll take you home."

And that was all she could promise. She squeezed her eyes shut. *This is how Noah felt,* she thought. *Hamstrung and useless.*

"Helena, you're going to get through this," she added, running her hand over Helena's disheveled hair. She couldn't offer the weeping woman anything beyond survival. They could take her away from here. They could deliver her to her friends and family. But no one could change the past or guarantee that Helena wouldn't spend the rest of her life looking over her shoulder, waiting for her past to tear her apart all over again.

Maybe Helena will be stronger. Maybe she'll break free from the past.

Caroline felt her own tears hot against her cheeks as Helena's fingers pressed into her skin.

Or maybe we're both out of second chances.

CAROLINE WIPED AWAY one last tear as she leaned against Helena's Mercedes-Benz. She'd backed the car out of the garage while the woman they'd come to rescue spoke to the officers. Despite her initial rush onto the scene, Caroline was trying to stay in the background. But she couldn't exactly jump in the pristine hedges and hide every time an officer walked by her. Cops now swarmed the yellow mansion.

Standing on top of the redbrick stairs, just outside the front door, Helena nodded to the officers. She motioned for Caroline to join them. She walked over and placed her hand on Helena's still-trembling arm.

"We'll need to speak with you again in the morning, Mrs. Watterson," an older man with a weathered face and grey-green eyes said. He wore plain clothes, a black polo and khakis. He'd arrived after the first two officers in uniform—the ones who'd caught hold of Mr. Ashford Watterson when he'd taken a swing at Josh—had radioed for backup. With his gentle smile and tall build, the officer in charge reminded Caroline of Josie's dad, Forever's police chief.

"If you change your mind about seeking medical attention," the officer added. "Or a rape kit—"

"No," Helena said firmly. "I want to leave, to get away from here."

The officer nodded. "I understand. I still need to ask you some questions in the morning."

"If it's all right with you, sir," Josh said, speaking directly to the Josie's dad look-alike, "my friend here will take Mrs. Watterson back to our hotel. We're a five minute drive away. And we can bring her to the station in the morning—or the hospital."

The officer nodded and held out a business card to Helena. "Call me if you need anything, ma'am."

She nodded and moved to Caroline's side. Helena took her hand. Together, they headed for the Benz.

"I'll need her name for the report," the lead cop said. "Your friend's name."

Caroline stumbled on the brick path to the driveway. *Her name.* Oh hell, this was it. If they ran her identity, they'd find the warrant. She would be arrested—maybe not tonight, but in the morning.

She glanced at Helena. Even after all she'd been through, after what Caroline had heard through the open phone line, the other woman held her chin high.

If I end up in a cell . . . it was worth it.

The trip, the series of dates, and their crazy, poorly planned rescue—if she lost her freedom in the morning, it would all have been worth it. She'd taken a chance. She'd made love to a man whom she loved. And she'd helped someone who needed her as much as she'd needed Noah. Maybe she hadn't been able to save herself and find the number for the hotline while stationed in the middle of nowhere in Afghanistan. But she'd saved Helena tonight.

It's worth it.

Caroline glanced back at Josh.

Even if I lose him.

Her heart hiccupped. She'd fallen for Josh Summers and she didn't want to walk away.

"Caroline?" Helena murmured.

She turned away from Josh. Love wasn't enough. She took another step toward the parked Benz. As soon as Josh gave the officer her name, her second chance would crash and burn. Her happy-ever-after had been stripped away long before now, when she'd given in to fear and run away. Josh, their love, and their future—it had been impossible from the start.

Settled into the driver's seat, Caroline took one last look at the redhead with the tempting smile chatting with the lead cop. She'd fallen for Josh. But what kind of future would they have if she stayed in hiding?

She put the car in reverse, looked over her shoulder, and guided the Benz down the drive. Failure had been closing in on her from the beginning. And there was only one thing she could do to stop it.

"When we get to the hotel," Caroline said as she drove past the security gate, "I need to leave for a while. Before Josh gets back. You'll be safe and I don't think he'll be much longer."

"You're running away?" Helena said. "Now?"

"No, I'm done running."

"HER NAME? MY friend's name?"

Josh searched for the right answer. He couldn't give Officer Peters the truth. He glanced over at the driveway and watched as the Benz backed out with Caroline at the wheel.

You can trust me to keep your secret safe.

He turned his attention back to the police officer. Josh

offered a faint smile. "My friend's name is Josie Fair— No, sorry, she's Josie Tager now."

He'd keep her secret all right. And he'd make an ass of himself while he spit out a simple little lie.

"She's recently married?" the officer asked as he scribbled in his notepad.

"Yes. Josie just tied the knot. But not to me," Josh explained with a laugh. "We're just friends. I volunteered to drive her down here. To see her friend."

The police officer nodded.

"So," Josh said, clapping his hands together. "How much longer will you need me?"

Thirty minutes later, Josh pulled into the hotel garage, put his truck in park, and glanced down at his phone. Midnight. He should call Big Buck's and fill Noah, Dominic, and whoever else was at the bar in on what had happened tonight. But instead, he climbed out of his truck and pocketed his phone.

Later, he decided. First, he needed to see Caroline, hold her, and make damn sure she was all right. He bypassed the hotel's elevator bank in favor of the stairs. He took them two at a time until he reached the door to the fourth floor. It had been hard to get away from the cops and their questions or he would have been here before now to reassure her that he hadn't shared her name or her secret.

He'd lied for her. And he would maintain the charade, here and at home, whatever she needed to feel safe and stay in his life. He wouldn't lose her. Not to her past or anything else. They could pretend and lie to the rest of the world—in his heart he knew the truth.

He slipped his card key into the door and opened it to the room. "It's Josh," he announced as he stepped inside. He spotted Helena in the black desk chair. She held a tiny bottle of wine that looked as if it had come from the room's mini-fridge. Another bottle sat on the desk, empty.

"Celebrating?" he asked as he glanced to the bathroom door. It was open. But there was no sign of Caroline.

"She left," Helena said.

"Caroline went out?" He turned back to the woman they'd helped. He wouldn't say 'rescued' because Caroline had been right, Helena had saved herself. "If I'd known you ladies were hungry, I would have stopped and picked something up on my way back."

Helena pressed her lips together. She'd scrubbed off the makeup and looked years younger and a lot more vulnerable. "No, she called a cab. But she wrote you a note."

Numbness descended. His body felt as if he'd been plunged into the Pacific's icy waters without a wet suit. But he managed to walk across the hotel room, past the spot where Caroline had . . .

Fuck, he couldn't picture her on her knees. He couldn't go backward through the memories, searching for a clue until he knew what the hell was going on. He took the folded piece of paper from the tipsy Helena and turned his back to her.

Flipping it open, he started to read. And shit, one sentence in and he needed a shot of something—whiskey, vodka, or liquid rage—anything to dull the damn pain of his heart shattering.

Dear Josh,

By the time you get this, I will be at the police station.

Fuck, fuck, fuck . . . He'd been dodging failure, trying to navigate their complicated relationship like it was a damn minefield from the beginning. He'd worried her problems were too big and he'd been right.

He looked down at the paper and forced himself to keep reading.

It's time that I turned myself in and faced the consequences for running away from my duty to serve. Until I do, I will never have a chance at getting my life back on track. I can't ask you to love me and lie for me without dooming our relationship. You said something always happens next. And this is what's next for me.

I'm ready now to face my punishment. I will return to my unit if I have to, accept a demotion or serve my time in prison. But I will not let anyone make me feel like I need to be less ever again. I know now what happens when I push past 'impossible.'

I fall in love.

I love you, Josh Summers. But don't you dare wait for me. Go back to Oregon and build your house. Take another chance on finding happiness. I'd hate to think we're limited to two shots. If we are, then I've used mine up. And that, more than anything, feels impossible.

Love,
Caroline

PS: Take care of Helena. Try to talk her into the
rape kit. The police need all the evidence they can
·get. Then bring her back to Forever. And when you
get there, tell Noah I said thank you, but this time I
needed to break free from my past on my own.

Josh stared at the note and read it through a second time, then a third. And the silence in the room, the lack of laughter and of Caroline's wry humor, the too-serious tone of the letter—it all added up to one sad truth. She was really gone.

He'd let a woman walk out of his life once before. Sure, he'd been a kid then. But he'd never tried to find his mom. He'd given up, accepted the hit, and moved on.

Not this time.

"When did she leave?" he demanded, turning to Helena.

"One bottle of wine before you returned?" Helena held up the empty minibar bottle that he'd spotted on the desk.

Shit.

"Can you stay here?" he asked. "Will you stay *right here* and wait for me to go get her?"

She nodded. "I might pass out."

"The bed's all yours. Just whatever you do, don't run." After this, after he found Caroline, he was done chasing women.

JOSH PULLED INTO the police station parking lot. He'd tried the one closest to the hotel first, but she wasn't there. He'd run into Officer Peters, the lead detective from their earlier adventure at Helena's house. He'd lied to the man earlier, but he didn't stop to explain that now. He'd begged the officer, who looked a helluva lot like Josie's dad, to find out if an AWOL Marine had turned herself in tonight.

The minutes had ticked by, but Officer Peters had made a few calls and learned that another station had contacted the military police. A fugitive was being transferred from civilian to military custody tonight.

Josh hugged the man and bolted from the station. He'd sped across town, hanging on his phone's every instruction, and hoping like hell he got there in time. The one-story station house had a small, mostly empty parking lot. A black, unmarked sedan idled out front, but he didn't see signs of a Humvee. And that's what the military drove, not unmarked black cars sent out in the middle of the night . . .

But as he climbed down from his truck, the door to the station swung open. Two men in uniform—one short, maybe five-six in his boots, and another tall and built like a tank that refueled on fried food and sugar— marched through the door. They each had one hand on a petite woman with long dark hair. Even with her hands behind her back and her head down, she looked like she had that first night in the Oregon woods—a little wild and very fierce.

"Caroline," he called. He spotted a third driver now, ready and waiting to take her away. He broke into an all-out run. "Caroline, please!"

"Let me go, Josh," she called as the soldiers flanking her sides hustled her down to the waiting car. "I'm sorry, but I need to do this. I can't keep hiding."

"I'm going to find a way out," he said as he moved closer. "Trust me, Caroline."

The man on her right, the smaller of the two, opened the door to the backseat. And for that second, while she stood still, her gaze met his. And he saw her uncertainty. She trusted him in the bedroom. Now he needed her to have faith that he wouldn't let her go without a fight.

The shorter soldier held the car door open. "Let's go," he said.

Josh saw a flash of metal as they turned her and guided her into the vehicle. *Handcuffs.* After everything she'd been through and endured while serving her country, they had the woman he loved, the woman he wanted to build a life with, in cuffs.

The injustice ripped at him.

"I'm sorry, sir," the larger of the two men said as he closed the car door to the backseat of the sedan and turned to face Josh. "We're only doing our jobs. And we don't want trouble."

Between the man's broad shoulders, square jaw, and military buzz cut, he looked like the poster boy for the Marines. Josh drew back a fist, ready to take a hit at the only target he had. But the Marine's poster boy simply raised his hands in a sign of surrender.

"Just doing our jobs," he repeated.

"She was raped," Josh bit out, letting his rage fill his words. "Did she tell you that? And the officer who attacked her, the asshole who drove her into hiding, the one who sent her running from her life so that she wouldn't have to deploy alongside the men who'd taken his side, *her rapist's side*, he's free. And you're taking *her* away in handcuffs."

The poster boy's lips parted and for a second he thought the Marine would pull open the door and set her free. But he just shook his head. "I'm sorry, sir."

The soldier took a step back and opened the passenger side door. And Josh felt his stomach turn over. They were taking her away. And hell, she was going with them. She wasn't fighting back or demanding release. She'd handed herself over.

For him.

So he wouldn't have to lie for her.

He just wished she'd waited and talked to him before she'd surrendered to the police.

"I love you, Caroline," he screamed into the night. The sedan picked up speed around the turn at the end of the parking lot, but paused at the exit to the road. And he could have sworn he saw the Marine in front crack his window.

"I love you," Josh called again. And then in a lower voice, "Please believe me . . . have faith in me, and in us . . . I won't let you down."

The car pulled onto the quiet two-lane road lined with street lamps. He watched until the sedan disappeared from sight. Then he turned and headed back to his truck. And he raised his fist, bringing it down hard against the driver's side window.

Watching the woman he loved be led away in handcuffs, he'd never felt so damn impotent. Like such a fucking failure. What the hell had gone wrong? Of all the time bombs waiting to blow up their relationship, he'd never imagined this. Why couldn't she have waited for him to come back? Talked to him? Trusted him with her fears? Believed that he'd stand by her and help her? Why did she have to make up her mind all on her own that this was the only way forward?

Slowly, he raised his head. He couldn't stay here. There was a terrified woman who'd been hurt badly waiting for him back at the hotel. And there was his life—and his family—back in Oregon.

He took one last look at the empty road.

And there was Caroline . . .

He pulled open the driver's side door and reached for his cell. It was two in the morning, but he knew someone would pick up.

"Big Buck's," Noah answered in a calm, collected tone that suggested the night's rush had come and gone.

Damn good thing because Josh needed the former Marine to jump into action.

"Caroline's in custody," he snapped. "I'm at the station now. The police just handed her off to the military. Marines, army police, I don't know who the hell they were, but they led her away in *handcuffs*." And yeah, his voice broke at the end. But dammit, the image was still too raw in his mind.

"You—"

"No, I didn't turn her in," Josh said, running a hand through his hair. "But you bet your ass I'm going to get her out."

He'd been right all along. Her problems were too big for him to tackle on his own. "Noah, I need you to do me a favor and call my brothers. I'm going to pick up Helena back at the hotel—"

"She agreed to come with you?" Noah said.

"She broke herself out," Josh said. "I'll give you the full story—or she will—when we get back. But Mr. Ashford Watterson is in custody and while Helena will probably still have to come back here to sort things out, I think you can go ahead and call Ryan. Tell him not to worry about her."

"I will," Noah said.

"We're heading back. Tonight," Josh continued as he climbed into his truck and put it in gear. "We'll be there in about nine hours. Can you have everyone at the bar?"

"You have a plan," Noah said.

"Not yet. But I'm not leaving Caroline to face this on her own. She doesn't believe me. Hell, I don't think she trusts that I can pull it off"—*and she might be right to doubt me*—"but I'm going to get her back. What's happening to her, it's not right."

"No, it's not," Noah said. "And Josh? You don't have to do this alone."

"Thanks." He ended the call and focused on getting back to the hotel. The sooner he picked up Helena, the sooner they could get on the road to Oregon.

And find a way to get Caroline out of those damn cuffs. *No escape.*

Her words echoed in his memory. Maybe she believed that, but he wasn't going to give up. He'd find a way to get her out. He'd get her another shot at freedom.

Chapter 18

CAROLINE STARED STRAIGHT ahead. She blocked out the sounds around her—the radio, the soldiers' voices, the click of the turning signal as the car merged onto the highway. None of it mattered. All she had to do now was focus on getting through this.

She had narrowed her focus and shut down her senses on the taxi ride to the police station. Her heart, her feelings—she'd spelled those out for Josh and handed the slip of paper to Helena. Then she'd taken her wallet with her identification and she'd walked out the door. Her gun, her backpack, and everything else she'd carried with her on this trip, including her black lace undies, had stayed behind.

She needed to survive. There was nothing more now.

No escape.

She felt the urge to turn around and look out the back of the sedan into the dark night. She wanted one more glimpse of him. But she knew they'd already traveled too far.

Still, she hadn't expected Josh to find her. She'd avoided the nearest police station, knowing he'd look there first. And she hadn't steeled herself for his words.

Trust me.

Oh, she'd heard every word he'd fired at the soldiers tasked with transporting her to the nearest military base. She'd listened as he jumped to her defense and she'd soaked up his every *I love you.*

But when he'd asked her to have faith in him, to believe that he would fix this . . . she'd faltered.

How could he help her now? She didn't even know where they were taking her. She hadn't asked how soon she would be court-martialed. Or which military prison was nearby. She had no idea what would happen to her next.

Something always happens next.

He'd been right about that. And this was the only step left for her—this bleak, heartbreaking path.

She closed her eyes and beat back the tears. She'd wept once tonight. For Helena. And she'd opened her heart to a spectrum of emotions while she wrote that letter.

Now it was best to remain numb. If she let herself feel, the despair would rush in.

But no matter what happened next, no matter where they took her, or what sentence they handed down for her unauthorized absence, she was done living in fear.

JOSH PULLED INTO the Big Buck's parking lot at two in the afternoon the next day, a full twelve hours after he'd called Noah. He was surprised to find the bar closed. The lights were off. And as he climbed out of his truck, he saw a sign hung on the door that read 'Closed for Emergency Repairs.'

It had taken him longer than he'd expected to get back to the hotel in Palo Alto, rouse a passed out Helena, and get on the road. Plus, when they'd arrived in Forever he'd agreed to drop his hungover and exhausted travel companion at her mother's house. Helena had been through enough in the past twenty hours and he wasn't about to subject her to an interrogation. Plus, he knew her childhood friends would have a mountain of questions.

He walked past the line of familiar cars and pickups. He raised a tired hand and knocked on the wooden door beside the sign. Noah pulled it open, propped the door with his foot, and folded his arms across his chest.

"About damn time you got back here." He nodded to the long wooden bar and scattered high top tables lined with familiar faces. "We got started without you."

Josh stepped into Big Buck's and surveyed the space. His gaze landed on Brody and Chad. His brothers shared a table with Kat, the doctor who'd helped Josh reclaim his memory—and in the process fallen for his oldest brother—and Lena, the army veteran who never left the house without her golden retriever, Hero. Right now, her PTSD service dog sat at her feet chewing on his toy duck.

"Before you start," Josh said, pointing a finger first

at Brody and then at Chad, "I love her. This is it for me. I'm not trying to win her back just because she walked out. I'm not playing out some messed-up 'abandonment issues' or anything."

"Didn't say you were," Chad muttered, but one look from Brody and their middle brother shut up.

"I'm not trying to slot her into some version of my fantasy future," he added.

His eldest brother raised an eyebrow.

"OK, maybe at first, I was looking to make the pieces fit. But not anymore." This earned an approving nod from Kat.

"And I'm sure as hell not trying to be a hero," Josh continued, looking away from his brothers and scanning the room. "I can't do this on my own. I need your help because . . ."

He shook his head. He couldn't believe he was standing here in front of his family and the Big Buck's crew spilling his guts. "I need your help because I'm so damn afraid I'm going to let her down. And she's not just my second chance after all the shit I've been through . . . the accident, the coma . . . She's my everything." His voice broke over that last word, but he kept going. "And I'll use up all my chances to get her back."

"We're going to get her out," Noah said, slapping Josh on the shoulder as he walked past. "While you were driving back, we started making calls."

"I found a therapist who specializes in military sexual trauma," Kat announced. "She's based in Washington, DC, but she's willing to fly out here to meet with Caroline. She's respected in the military community. I think we can get her access if we make some noise."

"We have a plan for that," Lily piped up.

"And I spoke with my counselor," Lena said as she lowered her hand to her dog. "There's precedence for a medical discharge. Women who suffer from MST or even PTSD have been released without jail time before. Even after they've gone AWOL. If we can pull some strings, she would avoid being court-martialed."

"Pull some strings?" Josh repeated. How the hell was he going to manage that?

"We have a plan for that too," Chad said. "We're going to call everyone who will talk to us. Reporters, representatives—"

"And friends who are still serving," Noah jumped in. "Josie's talking to her dad right now and seeing if he can help even though Caroline has already been handed over to the military police. Ryan is jumping at the bit to do you one helluva favor after what you did for Helena. Once we tell him what we need, he'll do it."

"We're going to get her out of there before anyone lays a finger on her," Dominic said. "You can count on it."

Josh stared around the room at all the determined faces and his fear slipped away. He wasn't going to let her down. He couldn't fail—not this time—because if he tripped up there would be someone—friend or family—waiting to pull him up. They were all on her side.

"Where do we start?" he asked.

Chad grinned. "How do you feel about pouring out your heart on national TV?"

Chapter 19

CAROLINE WALKED OUT of the barracks and silently cursed her surroundings. She'd been here for a handful of days and still hated everything about the base. She stared straight ahead and wondered if the California sun was playing tricks on her. She raised her hand to block the powerful rays, fully expecting the mirage to disappear. But he was still standing there, one ankle crossed over the other. His shoulder rested against the wall of her temporary home.

"Noah?" she said. "What are you doing here?"

He pushed off the wall and gave a small shrug. "I thought you could use some company on your day off. You're not working today, right?"

"I'm not but—"

"Join me for lunch."

"You drove all the way down here to take me out to lunch?" She narrowed her gaze. "There's not much around here. We're hours from the ocean."

And civilization, she thought.

Or at least she thought they were. She hadn't paid attention on the drive, slipped back into numbness.

"It took me twelve hours to get here. So I'm not dying to get back in my truck. I have a couple of sandwiches that I picked up just in case you had a break. Want one?"

"Sure." She followed him, feeling as if she'd traveled back in time. She was wearing her uniform and walking beside Noah. "What are you doing here?" she asked.

"Checking up on you," he said. "Seeing how you're holding up with all that's going on."

She stopped beside his truck. "Noah, I don't have a clue what is happening. I've been here for four days and I keep expecting a court-martial. According to every rule and regulation, I should be in a military prison right now."

"You should." He opened the driver's side door and retrieved a brown paper bag from the driver's seat.

"Instead I was assigned a room in the barracks and a desk job." She followed him to a nearby picnic table and claimed one of the benches. He sat on the other side and opened the bag.

"Hard work?" he asked as he handed her a six-inch sub.

"I don't have any responsibilities. I report for work and I sit there."

"And you have no clue why you're hanging out at a desk?" he challenged.

She shook her head.

"Didn't trust Josh when he said he'd find a way out, did you?" he asked.

"Josh?" She set her sandwich down before she dropped it onto her lap. Across from her, Noah unwrapped his sub and took a bite.

"It's not that I didn't believe in him," she said. "I trust him as much as I trust anyone . . ."

Maybe more in the bedroom, she thought. But she wasn't sharing the intimate details of her relationship with Noah. Not over subs on some out-of-the-way Marine base in God Knows Where, California.

Noah raised an eyebrow and took another bite.

"But how could Josh stop the United States Marine Corps from tossing me in a cell for unauthorized absence?" she demanded.

"After you turned yourself in," Noah said, his blue eyes flashing with temper. "Without so much as a word to anyone I might add."

"I'm sorry," she said. "I couldn't hide anymore."

He sat back and crossed his arms in front of his chest. "I know. But that man cares about you. And I'm not stupid, Caroline. I know Josh didn't take a scenic little road trip with you so that he could be your personal baker."

"What happened to staying out of my relationship with Josh?"

"He gathered us all at the bar. Dominic and Lily. Josie. His brothers. Brody Summers's wife. Hell, even Lena showed up. And he asked for help. He refused to accept failure as an option."

Her lips parted as she imagined all of those familiar faces gathered around the bar. "I don't even know his older brother," she murmured.

"Look, I know you went through hell. And starting over with a guy, even a good guy like Josh . . ." Noah raised his hands and ran them through his short, blond hair.

"Did you draw the short straw? Is that why you're sitting here and not Josie or Lily?"

"No, I didn't draw the damn short straw," he snapped, lowering her hands. "No one else knows I'm here. I woke up before dawn to come down here because Josh Summers is busting his ass to keep you out of jail. He's called senators and spoken to legal experts. He's fighting for you. He's trying to win your love and your trust, but if you can't give it to him, you need to tell him. Or shit, I will."

She arched an eyebrow. "You're offering to break up with my boyfriend for me?"

"Caroline," he growled.

"I'm not broken, Noah. And Josh knows that." She looked down at her untouched sub. "But I messed up. I should have talked to him before I turned myself in. I let him into every other part of my life . . ." She looked up. "I thought I had to fix this first. Before I could have another shot at falling in love. I didn't think I could give him what he wanted until—"

"Caroline, that man wants *you*. And if you're sure you're ready to move on, then you should probably tell him, not me."

"You're not going to relay the message for me?" And she couldn't help adding a healthy dose of sarcasm to her words.

"I like the guy. And after everything he's done for you . . . Do you know he went on a local morning show talk show and baked a cake with the host so that he'd have a chance to raise public support for you?"

"He what?" Panic rushed at the thought of thousands of people in Oregon knowing she'd been attacked—and seeing her as a victim.

"He didn't use your full name or broadcast your picture," Noah assured her. "But he told your story. And people listened. There is a petition demanding your release. Josie showed it to me. Josh kept Dustin's name out of it too—"

"He's not coming after me." She shook her head and filled him in on her drive-by visit to their former CO.

"Hell, I wish Josh would turn the media's attention to him," Noah grumbled. "But he's not. Josh is attacking the system that is threatening to lock you up while Dustin goes free. That's a lot to take on."

"He loves me," she said softly.

"And he'd willing to fight for you," Noah said.

She closed her eyes and nodded. She was haunted by her own choices. But this time—if she got the chance—she would choose Josh. She wanted to be a part of his happy-ever-after.

"He's going to get me out of here, isn't he?" she said.

Noah nodded. "Probably sooner than you think."

She fought the urge to hear those words and think *impossible*. She would put her faith, her love, and her trust in him.

"Noah, I need to be ready for him." She drew a deep

breath. "You've done so much for me already, but I have to ask for more. I need an advance on my paycheck. Probably a couple paychecks."

"Done." He smiled across the picnic table. "I'll even toss in a promotion to part-time bartender when you get back."

"Thank you. I don't know how to mix drinks, but thanks."

"You'll learn." He shook his head. "You can't be any worse than Lily."

She rested her arms on the table. "Now, I need to ask one more favor."

CAROLINE TOOK A tentative step forward. After weeks of walking around this base with purpose and determination, carrying her faith that Josh would come through for her around like a secret weapon, she felt nervous.

Is it really over?

She glanced down at the piece of paper detailing her medical discharge from the Marines. After spending over a year hiding, feeling hunted by her past, it was officially behind her. The Marines were done with her. And she had the man leaning against a familiar silver pickup to thank.

She wanted to run to him. She needed to weep with relief. But not yet. Right now she had to savor this feeling.

This is what freedom feels like. Scary. New. Exciting.

Oh yes, the tears could wait until much, much later. Right now, she needed to share her gratitude, her relief, and her love with the man who'd set her free.

"You're here." She crossed the parking lot, the base becoming a blur behind her. She'd spent days, weeks trying not to feel, and now . . .

Emotion erupted as if a faucet had been turned on. Her pulse raced and tears burned paths down her cheeks, refusing to wait. So she broke into a run. She needed to feel his hands on her, his arms around her. She wanted to hold on to him and never let go.

But first, oh God, she had to tell him.

"I'm sorry I didn't trust you." The words came out in a rush as his arms wrapped around her. She placed her palms flat against his chest and looked up at him. Ever since Noah's visit two weeks earlier, she'd been planning her speech. She refused to write him another letter. She needed to tell him.

"I should have told you that I was going to turn myself in," she continued.

"Caroline." His hands roamed over her waist and hips before settling on her lower back. "I know you're sorry. Noah told me."

Her eyes widened. "He did?"

"We had a sleepover, ate one too many cinnamon rolls, one thing led to another and he told me everything."

She laughed and it felt so good and so right. "Josh—"

"All right. We skipped the sleepover. And I didn't bake for him. But we did have a few shots of whiskey the other night." His smile faded and his hands stilled on her back. "I owe you an apology too. For the past year, I told myself I was giving you space and working around your issues."

"You did, Josh," she murmured, trying to fight a fresh

wave of tears. She was free and he was here, holding her. She didn't want to cry.

"But I have one question for you," she said quickly, reaching for facts to keep the feeling from running away with her. "If Noah found his way down here, why didn't you? Too busy making TV appearances?"

"That's part of it." He touched his mouth to hers, stealing a quick kiss. "I've also been poring over this mysterious set of blueprints that arrived."

She stared up into his green eyes. "You figured out they were from me?"

He let out a laugh as his hands pressed into her back, drawing her closer. "The architect that you hired dropped them off at the farmhouse," he said. "He wanted to walk me through them."

"Actually Noah hired him for me," she murmured, arching her lower back. Her chest pressed against his and her thigh brushed his.

I'm never letting you go, she thought.

"And was the 'Superhero's Lair' in place of a master bedroom Noah's idea too?" he asked, running one hand up her spine. His fingers brushed the bare skin at the nape of her neck and she felt a rush of pleasure.

"I might have sent a few suggestions," she said softly. But they could talk blueprints later. Right now, she wanted to touch him.

She ran her hands up to his shoulders, over his neck to his jaw. The red-gold stubble brushed against her palms as she drew his mouth to hers. With his lips hovering over hers, she added, "I don't want to hold you back from your dreams. I want to be a part of your happy-ever-after. I want to build that house with you. Set up our lair together."

She rose up on her toes and kissed him. Her tongue swept into his mouth, tangling with his. And she felt every inch of his excitement.

Slowly, she drew her lips away from his, but she kept her body close. Her back arched as she looked up at him. "We might want to start the road trip home soon. I think it would be a good idea to get off the base before we find out how much trouble we can get into in the front seat of your truck."

"I'm not taking you home." He grinned down at her. "Not yet."

"I recognize that look," she murmured. *And I trust that smile.* "You have a plan."

"I would have come down to visit you," he said, releasing his hold on her and she instantly wanted to climb back into his arms. But he reached into his jacket and withdrew an envelope. "I didn't want to settle for an afternoon," he continued. "I wanted to take you away with me." He held out the envelope. "These are for you. Go ahead."

She took the blue packet, opened it, and peeked inside. "Airplane tickets?" She pulled them out, her eyes widening as she read the details. "We're going to Hawaii? Tonight?"

"I packed a bag for you." He nodded to the truck. "And don't worry, I grabbed your black undies. But your gun had to stay in the safe."

"You planned a trip for me," she murmured, staring down at the tickets. "In between starting petitions to keep me out of a military jail cell, going on national TV, demanding meetings with senators, hiring lawyers—"

"Noah kept you informed"

She nodded. "You did all of this for me."

"For us. Plus I have this rule." His fingers touched her cheek and she looked up at him, her fingers still clutching the tickets. "I need to spend the sixth date with the woman I love—the beautiful, brave, fierce woman I've fallen *in love* with—on an island."

"I love you too, Josh Summers."

"I know, Caroline." His smile faded, but his eyes still sparkled with amusement. "But you know, I still haven't received a rose."

"I have a rule about that." She tried to match his pseudo-solemn expression—and failed. "No roses until the hot tub date."

"It's a damn good thing there happens to be a private one waiting for us in Hawaii, my love."

Epilogue

THE LANDLINE IN the private beachfront villa rang and rang. Caroline held her hands behind her back, twirling her final surprise between her fingers. The ringing stopped and she smiled, counted to five and . . .

Ring! Ring!

"Don't answer that," Josh advised from the bathroom's arched doorway. He rested his forearm against the entryway and offered a wicked, too-tempting grin. One day in Hawaii and this man's mouth was already driving her crazy.

Her gaze headed south. She followed the trail of red-gold hair down his taut abdomen, past the hard lines she'd explored with her mouth, tracing her way down until she'd slipped below the towel slung low around his hips.

Ring! Ring!

"What if it's Brody? He might be calling to tell you that their adoption was approved."

"It's not. I spoke to my big brother earlier. No news about their little girl. But they're confident it will come through soon."

He lowered his arm and stepped into the room. A wooden platform bed with an elaborately carved headboard filled the space to his left. The white sheet formed a tangled mess in the center. Beyond the bed French doors led to a secluded patio.

And one very big, very private hot tub.

Ring! Ring!

"Maybe it's Chad?" she murmured.

Josh shook his head and took another step, like a big, beautiful, red-haired lion stalking his prey. Her pulse sped up and she tightened her hold on her surprise.

"Chad should be in a helicopter right about now." Josh cocked his head and took another step. "Although I wouldn't put it past him to keep calling just to annoy me."

Ring! Ring!

"Katie?" she suggested.

"I talked to her when we landed. She's fine and still pregnant." He rose up his tiptoes and tried to peer over her shoulder. "Did you find a bikini? The hot tub on the patio is ready and waiting for us."

She stepped back until her fingers brushed a row of bamboos stalks in a decorative vase by the villa's front entrance. "No bikinis. But I might be willing to relax my rule about wearing swimsuits on our very private patio."

Ring! Ring!

"Someone really wants to talk to us. It might be Noah or Dominic."

"They can wait," he said firmly. "I sent a text to the Big Buck's group when we landed. They know you're free and we're taking a little vacation to celebrate. Noah will still have your job for you when you get back."

"I owe him a month's worth of shifts for covering the architect's bill." She twirled her present again. He'd slipped closer—

Ring! Ring!

"Who else has this number?" she wondered aloud. "The front desk? Did they accidentally give us a bungalow reserved for someone else?"

He shook his head. "No. This one is all ours." He glanced at the phone. In two long strides he was standing by the nightstand, bending over, and pulling the cables from the wall outlet.

"That's better."

She laughed. "But what if—"

"It's reporters, Caroline. The news about your release is spreading all over social media and TV." He glanced down at his bare feet and placed his hands on his hips. "I talked to a lot of people after you turned yourself in. I couldn't let them send you to prison. So I begged and I pleaded."

"I know." She closed the space between them and drew her hands around to her front. "That's why I choose you." She held out the single long-stem red rose.

"I left the competition in the dust?" He placed his hands on her hips and held her right there in front of him.

She drew a deep breath and tried to hide her smile. "There was no competition."

"Caroline," he murmured, following her lead and abandoning playful.

And she fought the urge to laugh. Instead, she brushed the tip of the rose over his bare chest down to the top of his abs. The muscles contracted, showing off and inviting more contact. She drew the rose down, down, down . . .

"Caroline," he growled.

"No competition," she said, her words soft, gentle, and heartfelt. No more teasing. Apart from the wicked rose pressed against his towel, begging to slip below the covering . . .

"Because you were the only man willing to push past impossible," she continued. "The one willing to wait until I trusted you."

His chest rose and fell with quickening breath and his grip tightened on her hips. She drew the rose lower, over the white towel to the hard, thick ridge beneath.

"The only one," she added, "willing to wait until I fell in love."

DESIRE ROARED THROUGH him and Josh fought the urge to pull her down to the bed and get lost in the tangle of sheets. They had a week to tear up the sheets. Longer if the reporters kept hounding them. He would stay here as long as they needed. Now that he had her back, he wasn't going to let her slip away again. If there were battles to fight, hurdles to cross, they would leap together.

And no more handcuffs. He released her hip and plucked the rose from her fingertips.

No more cuffs unless I put them on, he thought, amending his own edict.

But they could debate that rule—and which date fit best for bondage—later.

"Thank you." He raised the rose to his nose and pretended to take a long inhale. Peering over the top of the bud, he added, "You know what this means, don't you?"

"A one-on-one date?" she teased.

He nodded and tried to look serious. But hell, he hadn't been the solemn one in his family for a long damn time. And the woman who'd just handed him a rose knew it.

"Not just any date," he said. "A hot tub date."

He stepped back and took her hand. Then, still holding the rose in one hand, he grasped tight to hers and headed for the French doors.

"Time for some serious conversation," she added.

"Very," he agreed as he paused to toss the rose on the bed behind them. With his free hand, he pulled at the only thing covering his naked, eager body. His towel hit the floor and he opened the door. "How about I start while you undress?"

She let go of him and followed him out on the patio, pulling her shirt over her head as she walked.

"First, I'm going to start with your breasts. And I have a big decision to make. Should I press your tits together and dip my tongue between your breasts? Or—"

Her laughter drowned out his words and filled his heart.

"Save that conundrum for later? How about this." He held out his hand. "Come here, Caroline, and let me love you."

Don't miss any of the Second Shot novels! Keep reading for a look at the first in the series,

SERVING TROUBLE

Five years ago, Josie Fairmore left timber country in search of a bright future. Now she's back home with a mountain of debt and reeling from a loss that haunts her. Desperate for a job, she turns to the one man she wishes she could avoid. The man who rocked her world one wild night and then walked right out of it.

Former Marine Noah Tager is managing his dad's bar and holding tight to the feeling that his time overseas led to failure. The members of his small town think he's a war hero, but after everything he's witnessed, Noah doesn't want a pat on the back. The only thing he desires is a second chance with his best friend's little sister.

Josie's determined to hold on to her heart and not repeat her mistakes, but when danger arrives on Noah's doorstep and takes aim at Josie, they just might discover that sometimes love is worth the risk.

An Excerpt from
SERVING TROUBLE

"I DROVE TO the wrong bar."

Josie Fairmore stared up at the unlit sign tower-
ing above the nearly vacant parking lot, her cell phone
pressed to her ear. Nothing changed in Forever, Oregon.
Everything from the people to the names of the bars remained the same. The triplets, who had to be over a hun-
dred now, still owned The Three Sisters Café downtown.
Every car and truck she'd sped past had the high school
football team's flag mounted on the roof or featured on
the bumper. And her father was still the chief of police.

Nothing changed. That was why she'd left for college
and never looked back.

Until now.

She'd blown past the Forever town line ten minutes
ago. She'd driven straight to the place that promised a
rescue from her current hell. And she'd parked under

the sign, which appeared determined to prove her wrong.

"Josephine Fairmore, it is ten thirty in the morning," Daphne said through the phone, her tone oddly stern for the owner of a strip club situated outside the town limits. "The fact that you're at a bar might be your first mistake."

Damn. If the owner of The Lost Kitten was her voice of reason, Josie was screwed.

"When did they take the 'country' out of Big Buck's Country Bar?" Josie stared at the letters above the entrance to the town's oldest bar. She twirled the key to her red Mini, which looked out of place beside the lone monster truck in the lot. She should probably take the car back to the city. The Mini didn't belong in the land of four-wheelers, pickups, and logging trucks. The red car would miss the parking garage.

But I can't afford the parking garage anymore. I can't even pay my rent. Or my bills. . .

"Big Buck gave in three years ago," Daphne explained, drawing Josie's attention back to the bar parking lot. "He decided to take Noah's advice and get rid of the mechanical bull. He wanted to attract the college crowd."

"He got rid of the bull before I went to college." And before his son left to join the United States Marine Corps. She should know. She'd ridden the bull at his going away party.

With Noah.

And then she'd ridden Noah.

"Well, Buck made a few more changes," Daphne said. "He added a new sound system and—"

"He changed the name. I guess that explains why

Noah came home." She glanced at the dark, quiet bar. The hours posted by the door read "Open from noon until the cows come home (or 3am, whichever comes first!)."

"He served for five years and did two tours in Afghanistan. Stop by The Three Sisters and you'll get an earful about his heroics," Daphne said. "But from what I've heard, Noah didn't want to sign up for another five. Not after his grandmother died last year."

"You've seen him?" Josie looked down at her cowboy boots. She hadn't worn them since that night in Noah's barn. She'd thought they'd help her land the job at the "country" bar. But now she wished she'd worn her Converse, maybe a pair of heels.

"Yes."

"At The Lost Kitten?" Why, after all this time, after she never responded to his apologetic letter, would she care if Noah spent his free time watching women strip off their clothes? One wild, stupid, naked night cut short by her big brother didn't offer a reason for jealousy.

But the fact that I told him I love him? That might.

"No. I bumped into him at the café." Daphne hesitated. "He didn't smile. Not once."

"PTSD?" she asked quietly. She couldn't imagine walking into a war zone and leaving without long-lasting trauma. The things he probably saw . . .

"Maybe," Daphne said. "But he's not jumpy. He just seems pissed off at the world. Elvira was behind the counter that day. She tried to thank him for serving our country after he ordered a burger. He set a ten on the counter and walked out before his food arrived."

"He left his manners in the Middle East." Josie stared at the door to Big Buck's. "Might hurt my chances for getting a job."

"I think your lack of waitressing or bartending experience will be the nail in the coffin. But if Noah turns you down, you can work here."

"I'd rather keep my shirt on while I work," Josie said dryly.

And he won't turn me down. He promised to help me.

But that was before he turned into a surly former Marine.

"You'd make more without it," Daphne said. "Or you can tell the hospital, the collection agency—whoever's coming after you—the truth. You're broke."

"I did. They gave me a payment plan and I need to stick to it." She headed for the door. "I ignored those bills for months. Besides, what kind of mother doesn't pay her child's medical bills?"

The kind who buried her son twenty-seven days after he was born.

Daphne didn't say the words, but Josie knew she was thinking them. Her best friend was the only person in Forever who knew the truth about why she was desperate for a paycheck. If only Daphne had inherited a restaurant or a bookstore—a place with fully clothed employees.

"He has to agree," Josie added. "I need that money."

"I know." Daphne sighed. "And I need to get to work. I have a staff of topless waitresses and dancers who depend on me for their paycheck. Good luck, Josie."

"Thanks." She ended the call and slipped her phone

into the bag slung over her shoulder alongside her wallet and resume.

She drew a deep breath. But a churning feeling started in her belly, foreboding, threatening. She knew this feeling and she didn't like it. Something bad always followed.

Her boyfriend headed for the door convinced he was too young for a baby . . . Her water broke too early. . .

She tried the door. Locked, dammit.

Ignoring the warning bells in her head telling her to run to her best friend's club and offer to serve a topless breakfast, she raised her hand and knocked.

"Hang on a sec," a deep voice called from the other side. She remembered that sound and could hear the echo of his words from five long years ago, before he'd joined the Marines and before she'd gone to college hoping for a brighter future—and found more heartache.

Call, email, or send a letter. Hell, send a carrier pigeon. I don't care how you get in touch, or where I am. If you need me, I'll find a way to help.

He'd meant every word. But people changed. They hardened. They took hits and got back up, leaving their heart beaten and wrecked on the ground.

She glanced down as if the bloody pieces of her broken heart would appear at her feet. Nope. Nothing but cement and her boots. She'd left her heart behind in Portland, dead and buried, thank you very much.

The door opened. She looked up and . . .

Oh my . . . Wow. . .

She'd gained five pounds—well, more than that, but she'd lost the rest. She'd cried for weeks, tears running down her cheeks while she slept, and flooding her eyes when she woke. And it had aged her. There were lines on her face that made her look a lot older than twenty-three.

But Noah . . .

He'd gained five pounds of pure muscle. His tight black T-shirt clung to his biceps. Dark green cargo pants hung low on his hips. And his face . . .

On the drive, she'd tried to trick herself into believing he was just a friend she'd slept with one wild night. She'd made a fool of herself, losing her heart to him then.

Never again.

She'd made a promise to her broken, battered heart and she planned to keep it. She would not fall for Noah this time.

But oh, the temptation . . .

His short blond hair still looked as if he'd just run his hands through it. Stubble, the same color as his hair, covered his jaw. He'd forgotten to shave, or just didn't give a damn. But his familiar blue eyes left her ready to pass out at his feet from lack of oxygen.

He stared at her, wariness radiating from those blue depths. Five years ago, he'd smiled at her and it had touched his eyes. Not now.

"Josie?" His brow knitted as if he'd had to search his memory for her name. His grip tightened on the door. Was he debating whether to slam it in her face and pretend his mind had been playing tricks on him?

"Hi, Noah." She placed her right boot in the doorway, determined to follow him inside if he tried to shut her out.

"You're back," he said as if putting together the pieces of a puzzle. But still no hint of the warm, welcoming smile he'd worn with an easygoing grace five years ago.

"I guess you didn't get the carrier pigeon," she said, forcing a smile. *Please let him remember.* "But I need your help."

NOAH STARED AT the dark-haired beauty. Her white T-shirt hugged her curves, and her cutoff jean shorts sent him on a trip down memory lane. And those boots . . .

The memory of Josephine Fairmore had followed him to hell and back. He'd tried to escape the feel of her full lips, the taste of her mouth, her body pressed up against his . . . and he'd failed. He'd carried every detail of that night in the barn with him to basic training. Right down to her cowgirl boots. He'd dreamed about Josie in a bikini, Josie on the mechanical bull, Josie damn near *anywhere*, while hiking through the Afghan desert. He'd spent years lying in makeshift barracks wanting and wishing for a chance to talk to her while staring into her large green eyes.

And yeah, who was he kidding? His gaze would head south and he'd let himself drink in the sight of her breasts.

He closed his eyes. He'd spent two long deployments hoping for an email, a letter—something from her. He'd wanted confirmation that she was all right. But she never wrote. Not once. She'd reduced him to begging for tidbits from Dominic. Not that her brother had volunteered much more than a *She's fine. Stay the hell away from her.*

But she wasn't fine.

He opened his eyes.

"You needed help and you sent a pigeon?" He released his grip on the door and rested his forearm against it. "You could have called."

"I thought it would be better to apply for a job in person," she said, her voice low and so damn sultry that his dick was on the verge of responding.

Not going to happen.

There were a helluva lot of things beyond his control. His dad's health. His grandmother's heart failure while he was stationed in Bumblefuck, Afghanistan, fighting two enemies—and one of them should have been on his side. And the fact that the only time he felt calm, in control, and something bordering on happiness, was at the damn shooting range.

Still, he could control his own dick.

But why the hell should I?

He let his gaze drift to her chest, down her hips, and down her slim legs. He'd wanted her for five long years and here she was on his doorstep. What was stopping him from pulling her close and starting where they'd left off five years ago? He wasn't the good guy worried about her big brother's reactions or her reputation. Not anymore. Nothing he'd done in the past five years had left him feeling heroic. So why start now?

She crossed her arms in front of her chest. And while he appreciated the way her breasts lifted, he raised his gaze to meet hers.

"I'm not hiring," he lied. Big Buck's needed a waitress

or two, another bartender, and a dishwasher to keep up with the crowds pouring in from the nearby university, desperate to bump and grind to house music. But if she worked here, well hell, then he'd have another reason he shouldn't touch her. He had a rule about messing around with his female employees. It was bad business. He'd worked too hard to turn Big Buck's into something to fool around with a waitress or a bartender.

She raised an eyebrow and nodded to the Help Wanted sign he'd put up in the window. "Someone put that up without asking you?"

Shit.

"I recently filled the position," he said, searching for an excuse that didn't touch on the truth.

"I'm too late." She shook her head. "Perfect. I guess I should have gotten up the nerve to come home a few days ago."

He glanced over her shoulder and saw a red Mini parked beside his truck. It looked like a toy next to his F-250. And apart from the driver's side, every cubic inch appeared stuffed with bags.

"I thought you liked Portland. Greg from the station said you haven't been back here in a few years," he said, knowing he should close the door and end the conversation. If he let her in, if he handed her an application followed by a Big Buck's apron, he couldn't touch her. That wasn't much different from the past five years, or the ones before the going away party, but she hadn't spent the past decade or so within arm's reach.

"It didn't work out," she said.

"They don't have jobs up there for someone with a fancy degree? I bet you could do a lot better than serving drinks."

She blinked and for a second he thought she might turn around and walk away, abandoning her plea for help. "I took a break from school, lost my scholarship, and then dropped out," she said.

"What?" He stared at her. "Dominic never said—"

"My dad didn't know I'd quit school until recently. And I don't think he told Dom," she said quickly. "My brother has enough to worry about over there. Like not getting killed or . . ."

"Worse," he supplied. Like losing a limb or a fellow soldier. Yeah, Noah knew plenty of guys who'd lost both. But he'd worried about losing respect for the band of brothers serving with him because they'd flat out refused to treat the woman busting her ass alongside them with an ounce of decency . . .

Except Dominic would probably have stepped in and saved the woman before she was attacked. Josie's brother wouldn't let the situation get beyond his control and then try to pick up the pieces.

"There are worse things than dying out there," he added, trying to focus on the here and now, not the past he couldn't change.

"Yes."

He kept his gaze locked on her face as he stepped back and placed his hand on the door again. He was ready and willing to slam it closed. She could tempt and tease him, but he refused to take his eyes off her face. Hell, he knew better than to play chicken with her breasts. Right now, with the way he wanted her, he'd lose that game.

First, he needed some time to process. He wanted space to think about the fact that things hadn't worked out for her in Portland. He needed her to leave before he pulled her close, wrapped his arms around her, and offered comfort. Before he begged to know every damn detail about what had happened.

No, he needed her gone. Because he'd learned one big life lesson from his time with the Marines: he wasn't a hero. He couldn't let old habits take over, pushing him to save her. He wanted Josie's hands on him, her lips pressed against him ... not her problems dumped at his feet. And if Josie was back in the town that had insisted on labeling her wild, holding her solely accountable for losing her panties in a hay wagon ride, then something had gone horribly wrong in Portland.

"I'm sorry," he said. "I can't—"

"I need a job, Noah." She wasn't begging, merely stating a fact. But desperation and determination clung to her words. Never a good combination.

Noah sighed. "Do you have any waitressing or bartending experience?"

"Not exactly." She forced a smile as she uncrossed her arms and riffled through the worn black leather shoulder bag. She withdrew a manila folder and handed it to him. "But I brought my resume."

Propping the door open with his foot, he took the folder and opened it. He read over the resume and tried to figure out how a series of babysitting gigs related to serving the twenty-one-and-older crowd.

"You took a year off between working for these two families." He glanced up. "To focus on school?"

"No." Her smile faded. "I can serve drinks, Noah. I'm smart and I'm good with people. Especially strangers. And now that you've taken the "country" out of Big Buck's, I'm guessing the locals don't camp out at the bar anymore."

"Some still do." And they gave him hell for telling his dad to remove the mechanical bull. Five years and the people born and bred in this town still missed the machine that had put the "country" in Big Buck's Country Bar. Some dropped by to visit the damn thing in his dad's barn. But he'd bet no one had ridden it like Josie in the last five years.

He closed the folder and held it out to her. "Why are you so desperate to serve drinks?"

"I owe a lot of money."

Another fact. But this one led to a bucket of questions. "Your father won't help you?"

She shook her head. "This is my responsibility. He's giving me a place to stay until I get back on my feet."

The don't-mess-with-me veneer he wore like body armor cracked. If someone had hurt Josie . . . No, she wasn't his responsibility. Whatever trouble she'd found—credit card debt, bad loans—it wasn't his mess to clean up. He'd spent most of his life playing superhero, first on the football field, later for his family, and then for his fellow Marines. But his last deployment—and the fallout—had made it pretty damn clear that he wasn't cut out for the role.

He couldn't help Josie Fairmore. Not this time. And he sure as hell couldn't give her a job that would keep her underfoot. He couldn't pay her to work for him and want her at the same time. It wasn't right. Maybe he was a failed hero. But he still knew right from wrong.

"Look, I need experienced waitresses and bartenders." He stepped away, ready to head back to the peace and quiet of his empty bar.

"So you haven't filled the positions?" she asked.

"I—"

"Please think about it." She removed her foot, offering him the space to slam the door. "If you can't help me, I'll have to take Daphne up on her offer to serve topless drinks at The Lost Kitten. And I'd rather keep my shirt on while I work. But one way or another, I'm going to pay back what I owe."

She turned and headed for the red Mini. He stared at her back and pictured her bending over tables. One look at her bare chest and the guys at The Lost Kitten would forget what they planned to order. He hated that mental image, but jealousy didn't dominate his senses right now.

He'd witnessed a woman sacrifice her pride and her dignity for her job. He'd fought like hell for her and he'd failed her. He couldn't change the past. What happened to Caroline was out of his hands now. Even if he wanted to help, he couldn't. She'd disappeared. If and when Caroline resurfaced, she'd be the one charged with a crime. Unauthorized absence. And his testimony? The things he'd witnessed? It wouldn't matter.

But Josie was standing in his freaking parking lot.

"I'll give you one shot," he called. She stopped and turned to face him. Her full lips formed a smile and her eyes shone with triumph.

"A trial shift," he added. "If you can keep up with a Thursday-night crowd, I'll consider giving you a job."

"Thank you," she said.

"Come back around four. And don't get too excited. Your babysitting experience won't help with a room full of college kids counting down the days until spring break."

He closed the door and turned to face the dark interior of his father's bar. Giving her a shot didn't make him a hero. But it would give him a chance to figure out why she needed the money.

And keep reading for an excerpt from Sara Jane Stone's second book in the series,

STIRRING ATTRACTION

When Dominic Fairmore left Oregon to be all he could be as an Army Ranger, he always knew he'd come back to claim Lily Greene. But after six years away and three career-ending bullets, Dominic is battered, broken, and nobody's hero—so he stays away. Until he learns Lily has been the victim of a seemingly random attack. He'll do anything to keep her safe . . . even go home.

Lily is starting to find a life without Dominic when suddenly her wounded warrior is home and playing bodyguard—though all she really wants is for him to take her. But she refuses to play the part of a damsel in distress, no matter how much she misses his tempting touch. He'll leave as soon as she's safe and Lily knows her heart will never heal.

But as attraction stirs to so much more, danger closes in. With more than Lily's heart at stake, Dominic can no longer draw a line between protecting Lily and loving her . . .

IF IT WASN'T *for Taylor Swift and chocolate brownies, I would be at home wearing size six jeans and enjoying the first Monday of summer break.*

Instead, the potent combination drove Lily to add an extra mile to her morning run. She turned up the volume on Swift's not-so-country album and jogged down Forever's familiar Main Street, trying to shake off the extra calories clinging to her thighs. If she kept going for another ten, maybe fifteen minutes, she'd end up in the park beyond the university. The well-maintained paths weaving through a manicured forest might distract from the fact that she hated running.

But I ate three large brownies at the end-of-year celebration yesterday.

Because who could say no to a six-year-old student with a plate of homemade double-fudge brownies? She might have followed her heart when she'd applied to teach kindergarten in her hometown when she graduated from college. But now, at the ripe old age of twenty-nine, this career was hell on her thighs and waistline.

Not that the kids shouldered all the blame. She'd turned to chocolate for comfort so many times over the past few years that she'd started to wonder if she should follow her father into rehab.

But it hadn't worked for him. He'd been arrested for driving under the influence. And this time the court had ordered him to rehab again. Not that he'd bothered to tell her. She'd received a call from his girlfriend of the moment with the news.

No, she doubted a twelve-step program to abandon chocolate would work for her. Plus, there were some times when she loved her curves. On those days, she welcomed the sugar rush, always promising to run the next day.

And other times . . . well, after struggling to care for her mother toward the end, the handful of reunions with Dominic, followed by the breakups—she'd kissed him goodbye more times than she wanted to count—hadn't she earned a treat? She'd rather have Dominic . . .

But he hadn't returned to Forever. And she'd buried her hope that he ever would after he took two bullets to the chest and one through his hand. He'd almost died in a war-torn country, then again in Germany while on the operating table. But it was the shot that had ripped apart his right hand that might bury him alive. He couldn't go back to the army. The rangers had kicked him out of the only group he'd ever wanted to join.

And he still hadn't come home.

Not to her.

He'd taken a break from his outpatient rehab to meet his niece after she was born. But he'd only stayed for a few days. Lily had been so caught up in school that she hadn't realized he was in town until he'd left again.

The traffic light turned green and she ran across the street, heading for the quiet park. The university students had mostly left for summer vacation. Plus, it was after nine in the morning on a Monday. Most of Forever's locals were at work. She ran past a mother pushing a stroller toward the park's swing set. In the distance, she could see another jogger.

Alone with Taylor Swift . . .

She picked up the pace, determined to push the extra calories clinging to her legs into exile. She had a date tonight with a man who wanted the same things out of life. Marriage. Children. A fellow teacher who wished to settle in Forever, not run away. Ted was the definition of "good man" even if he never tried to back her up against the wall and take her . . .

Stop comparing him to Dominic. Stop waiting for someone who has made it clear he is not coming back.

The playground disappeared from view. She followed the path through the trees. Glimpses of the university's buildings were visible through the bright green leaves, but nothing more. Rounding the bend, she saw a flash of red.

A man. Tall. Broad. Wearing a sweatshirt in June. Who did that? It was hot today even for a summer day.

He drew closer. Running toward her as if he knew her and wanted to say hello. He was moving fast. He was wearing a ski mask. In June . . .

And then he was on top of her.

She hit the pavement and fell back. He came with her. And oh God, he was hitting her. Over and over. She heard screams and hoped the sounds came from someone who would help her. A hit to the jaw. A punch to the gut, this one stinging. And then . . .

Silence.

She'd been the one screaming, her voice high-pitched and terrified. She'd been the one begging for help until the reality sank in. She was alone. In the trees. Out of sight.

"Please . . . stop," she whimpered, struggling to break free. But she wasn't strong enough.

"You ruined everything," a deep voice growled.

She kept her arms over her head, protecting her face. But through the gap she saw dark brown eyes peering at her through the mask.

His pupils are huge. He sounds . . . familiar.

And he looks crazy.

Of course he was. Sane people didn't attack strangers in the park. But who was he?

He hit her forearm and she closed her eyes. The pain distracted from trying to place him. Her arms stung as if she'd been covered in paper cuts. It didn't matter who he was, she just needed him to stop hitting her, stop hurting her . . .

The weight lifted, but the pain remained. She reached for her side. It was wet from his punches.

No, that's not right.

She lifted her palm and saw the blood. And she screamed, over and over, never stopping to breathe. Panic rushed in and held her captive. Her world was reduced to one word.

Help.

No one came. Fear took over, shifting her cries. Screw help. She didn't need a white knight. She needed power, strength, and someone who gave a damn about her.

Dominic.

She called his name. Her voice bordered on hoarse. She inhaled and tried again, staring up at the trees. The branches shifted in the light breeze as if mocking her. Sunbeams slipped through the leaves.

He's not coming.

Her ranger wouldn't rush to her rescue . . .

But he wasn't an army ranger anymore. He'd been injured, rehabbed, and released. And he still hadn't come back to her.

So she'd moved on.

She shouldn't be calling for Dominic. Her new boyfriend—the man who promised a future filled with gentle kisses, romantic adventures, and children. If she made it out of this park . . .

Ted.

She called his name to the trees. The leaves shook, spilling pockets of sunlight on the path. Ted specialized in teaching elementary school kids to read. He was a good man, a kind person . . .

Her vision blurred and the leaves above her merged

together. She needed help *now*. She rolled to her side and the pain shifted, but it didn't increase. More wasn't an option. She'd reached her threshold. There was agony and passing out. Those were her only choices

But before she tried to escape the pain, she needed to crawl into the open. She had to save herself. Dominic, Ted, the woman in the park—they weren't rushing to her rescue. She needed to pull herself into the open.

Slowly, she maneuvered onto her belly and raised her left arm. If she could crawl . . .

Dragging her bruised, battered, and possibly sliced forearm over the paved path, she pressed down and pulled her body forward. Her legs scrambled for purchase, but she couldn't find her way onto all fours.

Time distorted like it did when she visited the dentist, and the receptionist insisted on redefining the word "brief." But she made progress. Two slides forward, she saw something pink lying on the path. Her cell phone. She crawled closer and picked it up. Music still blasted from the headphones. She turned it over and—

No service.

"Stupid woods," she muttered. "Stupid park."

Still clutching the phone, she started dragging herself forward again. She reached the edge of the path and spotted her saviors. Two girls raced forward as if they'd eaten an entire pan of brownies last night. Or maybe they'd simply spotted her.

Help.

But the cry died before she could part her lips. Her vision blurred. And then—

Nothing.

About the Author

After several years on the other side of the publishing industry, **SARA JANE STONE** bid goodbye to her sales career to pursue her dream—writing romance novels. Sara Jane currently resides in New York, with her very supportive real-life hero, two lively young children, and a lazy Burmese cat. Visit her online at www.sarajanestone. com or find her on Facebook at Sara Jane Stone.

Discover great authors, exclusive offers, and more at hc.com.